Published by CatsEye Press

ISBN-10: 1492905216
ISBN-13: 978-149290-521-9

A CIP catalogue record for this
work is available from the British Library.

Also available as a Kindle ebook
ISBN-13 978-1-84396-250-2

Cover
Edwina Kelly Design

Illustrations
Paul Dunstan

Pre-press production
www.ebookversions.com

Introduction

In the early 1970s, Clare Druce co-founded the pressure group Chickens' Lib, which later incorporated the Farm Animal Welfare Network.

She has re-homed many ex-battery hens, delighting in watching them experiencing freedom for the first time; at last able to walk; to feel the sun on their feathers; and to build a nest and to perch comfortably after a lifetime of deprivation.

The fight against the cruelty of the battery cage for egg production is now global, and Clare has worldwide contacts within the animal rights movement.

Clare Druce now lives in West Yorkshire with her musician husband. She has two daughters and four grandchildren.

About battery cages

Since *Minny's Dream* was first published in 2004, the European Union (EU) has outlawed the 'barren' battery cage for laying hens. Sadly, a new version of the battery cage – commonly called the 'entriched' or 'colony' cage – is still permitted.

These new-style cages still prevent hens from expressing every one of their natural behavioural patterns, so you may be sure that Minny's message remains as urgent as ever.

World wide, billions of laying hens are kept in cruel confinement, with the majority still imprisoned in old-style 'barren' cages.

Dedicated to Karen Davis,
who works tirelessly to make all Minny's
dreams come true.

MINNY'S DREAM

Clare Druce

CatsEye Press

Chapter 1
Exciting News

"Move? To the country?"

Only a moment ago Paula Brown had been eating her cornflakes, still half-asleep. A moment ago it had been a quite ordinary Wednesday morning, in the middle of an ordinary school week. Then, out of the blue, her parents had come up with amazing news.

"You mean the *real* country?"

"Right next door to a farm," promised Mrs Brown, absently handing her daughter a piece of buttered toast. "And it's a lovely cottage. Only small, of course, and it'll need a lot doing, but just right for the three of us. Two bedrooms, a sweet little sitting room with real beams, not to mention a great big kitchen. And a most *wonderful* garden." When she thought about the garden a blissful smile lit up Mrs Brown's face.

"Hardly a garden, Mags," Paula's father said, pouring himself a second cup of coffee. "Not yet. The whole thing will need digging over. It'll be a question of starting from scratch."

"Oh I know, Des," agreed Mrs Brown, sighing. (Mr Brown did tend to be a wet blanket.) "I just meant it'll be a proper garden given *time*. But there's already the orchard, with masses of wild daffodils…"

"An orchard?" gasped Paula. "But orchards are absolutely huge!"

"Well, this one's only little, love, but there are apple trees, and two plum trees, and a damson. It'll be gorgeous in spring."

"Been neglected for years," commented Mr Brown. "Bags of hard pruning needed."

"Still, there's all that space!" Mrs Brown looked dreamy. "Just give it a

1

"...It's a lovely cottage. Only small of course,
and it'll need a lot doing, but just right for the three of us."

year or two, and you'll see. That half acre will be my little bit of heaven."

"Cool," said Paula. "Seriously cool!"

The Browns had lived in the same small flat since Paula was a baby. It was on the ground floor of a seven storey concrete block, beside a busy main road. Mrs Brown had the greenest of fingers, but for all those years she'd had to make do with three little window boxes. Passers-by would often stop to admire her brilliant displays of bulbs in spring, and petunias and geraniums later in the year.

Then one night last summer vandals had uprooted everything, leaving Mrs Brown's beloved flowers lying wilting on the pavement, and soil scattered far and wide. She'd burst into tears and said she hated the dirty crowded city, and the horrid kids who could do this sort of thing. The next morning Mr Brown had hardly spoken a word, and slammed the front door loudly when he left for work.

That evening Paula's parents had sat up late, talking, and they'd come to an agreement. The only solution to their problems was to move house.

"But what about school? And Dad's job? And yours, Mum? *Can* we move, just like that?" Now that Paula knew about the move she was desperate for answers.

"There's a very good school just five miles away, with a bus to take you there." Mrs Brown was eyeing her daughter closely, hoping the prospect of starting a new school, where she'd not know anyone, wouldn't upset Paula too much.

"Cool," said Paula.

"And this is another bit of good news," her mother went on cheerfully. "Your dad's arranged to work for your Uncle Ian, at his garage."

"Roll on the day!" said Mr Brown, draining the last of his coffee, and getting up from the table. "It can't come soon enough, for me."

"And you, Mum?"

"Oh, I'll be busy for a while, getting us settled in. But I've got my plans, don't you worry."

"So when can I see the cottage?" Paula persisted. "Today?"

"Of course not today," said her father. "Now, just get on with your breakfast, Paula, or you'll be late for school." Mr Brown hated anyone being late.

"Yes, but *when*?"

"Soon," laughed Mrs Brown. "It has to be soon, as it happens. We've got to be out of here in less than three weeks. The people taking over this flat are in ever such a hurry to be in."

"Why didn't you tell me about all this before?" Paula wasn't sure she liked the idea of her parents hatching hugely important plans behind her back.

"We were worried, in case it fell through," said her father.

"Fell through! What, the cottage?" Suddenly Paula sensed a catch in this fantastic idea of moving to the country. Come to think of it, it *did* all sound a bit too good to be true.

"No, love," explained her mother. "Not fall through... like... like... collapse! We just thought something might go wrong."

"Someone else might have got there first, for instance," said her father. "Cash in hand."

"We just didn't want to disappoint you. Now!" Mrs Brown tried to sound brisk, forcing herself to stop thinking about the hundreds of wild daffodils beginning to peep through the grass under the fruit trees in the orchard. "Your dad's right. Finish your breakfast, and get off to school. Just think what a lot you'll have to tell your friends. They *will* be surprised."

3

And Paula said nothing. Scary though the prospect of a new school was, she was thinking about the bullies who'd been tormenting her. Just as on every other morning this term, they'd be out there, waiting for her. But now, through a wonderful stroke of good fortune, she had a means of escape.

By the time Paula arrived home that afternoon the hall was full of cardboard boxes and her mother had started packing up their belongings.

How different the living room felt already, without the photos and vases, the books and Mrs Brown's collection of china dogs. Paula thought it had a surprised look. "All right," it seemed to be saying, "I can tell you've lost interest in me. Still, I did my best. Sorry if I wasn't good enough for you all."

"We'll have a bit of tea, Paula, and after that you can take a couple of those boxes and sort out your books. Put the ones you still want in one, and any for the charity shop in the other. And be sure to label them clearly!"

When Paula went to bed that night her bookcase, usually crammed to over-flowing, stood empty. Goodness, she thought, this move to the country is for real! For an hour she lay daydreaming, trying to imagine her new bedroom. Her mother had told her it had a sloping ceiling and a deep windowsill you could actually sit on and look out over fields, and the woods beyond.

How could she possibly wait all that time to see Orchard Cottage for herself? The next three weeks felt like for ever.

Mrs. Brown had the greenest of fingers, but, for all those
years, she'd had to make do with three little window boxes.

4

Chapter 2

At home in Orchard Cottage

"Thank heavens! We're in!" Mrs Brown sank down on the nearest chair, the only one not piled high with odds and ends. "Be a love and put the kettle on, would you, Des? We could all do with a cuppa." She was so tired her legs were positively throbbing.

"What about milk?" asked Mr Brown irritably (he was tired too).

"What about it?" snapped Mrs Brown.

"There's none left. Not after all those cups of tea for the removal men."

"We'll just have to borrow then. Next door's a farm. They'll have milk, surely." Mrs Brown sighed. "Des, would *you* go round and ask."

Mrs Brown didn't feel like introducing herself to neighbours. Not now, not with her hair all over the place and her face red and shiny from rushing around since seven o'clock that morning. "I'll put the kettle on, and Paula can be finding the mugs."

Mr Brown felt in his pocket for change. "Do we know what they're called?"

"Dredge," replied Mrs Brown. "The estate agent told me. His wife gets all their eggs there, apparently."

"That's a queer name." Paula had just clattered down the uncarpeted stairs that led straight into the kitchen. She'd been deciding where the bed should go, in her new bedroom. "I'm glad we're not called Dredge."

"Don't be silly, Paula," said Mr Brown. "They can't help their name, can they? Back in half a mo', then."

5

Paula watched her father as he made his way down the overgrown path, before letting himself out into the narrow lane that ran between Orchard Cottage and Folly Farm. As he approached the farmhouse, she could hear a dog's frantic barking. These were deep throaty barks. Barks suited to a very large dog.

"There don't seem to be any animals," Paula said thoughtfully. "No farm animals, I mean." All she could see from the kitchen window was a long row of low sheds beyond the farmhouse, and two tall metal objects looming over them. Around the sheds were areas of yellowing scrubby grass. "No cows or anything," she added.

"They'll be somewhere," said Mrs Brown vaguely. "I'm sure Dad will be able to borrow."

Reluctantly, she got up from her chair and filled the kettle, then started opening cupboards and closing them again, planning the new kitchen. Mr Brown had set the kitchen range going, and already a cosy warmth was beginning to radiate into the chilly room.

Suddenly Mrs Brown flung her arms wide.

"Here, love!" She gave Paula a big hug. "Aren't you glad we've left the dirty old city? Come on, let's celebrate!" And she twirled her daughter round and round, till they were both laughing helplessly, only stopping when they nearly tripped over a box of saucepans.

At that moment Mr Brown appeared, carrying a jug of milk.

"Were they all right about it?" asked Mrs Brown. She was out of breath from her exertions; she hadn't danced for years! "Friendly and everything?"

"All right, yes. Not exactly friendly though." Mr Brown looked put out. "Somehow I got the feeling they don't much like townies like us. Still, we'll not be living in *their* pockets."

"A pity, though," said Mrs Brown, who had hoped for pleasant neighbours.

"Never mind," said her husband. "What about that cuppa?"

So Paula's mother poured out three mugs of steaming tea and the Brown family gathered round the kitchen table in Orchard Cottage for the very first time, while outside the twilight faded to darkness. For a moment they sat quietly, listening. Apart from the distant hooting of an owl, all was silent. As Mr Brown commented, you could have heard a pin drop.

That night, Paula needed no reminders about getting to bed. She couldn't wait to snuggle under her duvet beneath the low, sloping ceiling. There were no curtains at the little window (Mrs Brown still had those to make) and for a few minutes she lay staring at the bright stars. But very soon, just as she was planning what she would do the next morning, Paula fell asleep. It had been a long, long day.

Chapter 3
Paula's discovery

The next morning Paula woke to the sound of a blackbird singing. She could see him, with his bright orange beak, perched on a branch of the twiggy old elderberry bush that grew right up to the window. This was better than traffic noise, better than the sound of busy footsteps hurrying by! All she could hear was the bird's complicated, joyful song, and the incessant twittering of countless smaller birds. Paula was imagining how her bedroom would look in a few weeks' time. Her father had promised to decorate it before making a start on the rest of the cottage, which was all very shabby.

The next morning, Paula
woke to the sound of a blackbird singing.

Paula climbed out of bed and straightaway put her slippers on. The floorboards were bare, with poking up nails that needed hammering in, and sharp splinters here and there. She opened the window as wide as it would go, and sat on the deep sill, gazing at the fields and woods. Already, spring leaves were beginning to touch the dark wintry trees with delicate shades of green.

But very soon the chill crept through her pyjamas, and Paula dressed quickly. The kitchen was directly below her bedroom, and she could hear her mother moving about, preparing breakfast.

Today was the very beginning of the Easter holidays. Two whole weeks ahead with nothing to do but explore!

"Paula, Mrs Dredge will be wanting her jug back. Be a love and take it round, will you?"

Paula and her mother had just finished their first breakfast in Orchard Cottage. Mr Brown had left for Uncle Ian's garage an hour ago, remarking that he mustn't on any account be late for work – especially on his first morning! He'd sounded excited, but a little worried too.

Mrs Brown had kissed him as he left, and whispered, "Good luck, Des love", then watched from the window as he made his way to the car, trying not to get his suit wet as he brushed past the overgrown bushes that grew on either side of the path.

"OK, I'll take the jug now." Paula wanted an excuse for a closer look at the farm. "The only thing is, I heard a dog barking at Dad last night, and it sounded really big." Paula was scared of dogs.

"Dad says it's safely chained up. Just don't go too near. Here's the jug. Thank Mrs Dredge very much, won't you?"

"Course I will," Paula promised. "See you."

The sky was pale blue with hardly a cloud in sight, and as Paula crossed the lane the early spring sunshine felt warm on her bare arms. She noticed a small gate, beside the main five-bar one, and guessed the big gate was only used to let tractors through, or the Dredges' car and Land Rover which were both parked in front of the farmhouse.

Then she saw the dog, a huge Alsatian, crouching beside a gloomy kennel. On hearing the click of the side gate it stood up and started towards her, barking ferociously.

Paula's heart began to thump uncomfortably. Forcing herself to keep calm, she estimated the full extent of the chain, and then skirted round the dog at a safe distance. As she approached the front door, an angry voice yelled: "Shut up, Prince!" and a woman appeared round the side of the house.

"That my jug? Just bring it round to the kitchen, will you, I can hear my phone ringing." And Mrs Dredge hurried back indoors, high heels tap-tapping on the concrete path. Feeling awkward, Paula followed her.

Already, she was disappointed. Nothing she'd seen so far looked in the least bit like a real farm! Despite the dull rows of sheds, Paula had still been hopeful. Surely, tucked away somewhere, would be the scenes pictured in all the books she'd looked at about the country, ever since she was little. *Somewhere*, there had to be a proper farmyard, with motherly hens tucking broods of fluffy chicks under their wings, pigs rooting happily in heaps of straw, and a few contented cows nearby. And maybe even one or two horses, patiently looking out over their stable doors.

"Give it here, then," hissed Mrs Dredge, who'd by now answered her phone. When she reached out for the jug with her free hand Paula noticed her long purple-painted fingernails. Altogether, Mrs Dredge was wearing what Mrs Brown would have described as far too much make-up and her jet black hair was piled high on her head, and kept in place with some large and very fancy combs.

Paula glanced around the kitchen. She could tell the farmhouse was very old, yet everything inside was bright and modern, and not at all homely. She hovered in the doorway, waiting to see if Mrs Dredge was about to finish her telephone conversation. She seemed to be discussing a delivery to the farm. Whatever it was, it sounded big. Paula was sure she heard tonnes mentioned.

Then she decided she might annoy Mrs Dredge if she hung around listening, just so she could say 'thank you', so she mouthed the words, and with a feeling of relief, turned away. Her father was right, these people didn't seem at all friendly.

Since there seemed to be only one dog to worry about, and he was at the front of the house, Paula decided to look for a different way out of the farm. If she continued on, rather than retracing her steps, she might find another gate and manage to avoid Prince. Better still, she might even find out what went on inside those mysterious grey buildings!

Keeping alert to the danger of unchained guard dogs, Paula crept along the side of the house in the direction of the rows of sheds. The nearer she got to them, the more she noticed a peculiar smell, a musty, sickly sort of smell, unlike anything she knew.

The whole area was deserted. The sheds had no windows, and all their doors were closed. Along the sides of each shed were strange shafts, each one with a greyish patch of dust around it. All was silent, except for a low humming sound that seemed to be coming from the shafts.

Suddenly a clanking, grinding noise made Paula's heart leap and a second later a man emerged from the end shed. He was wearing wellies and dirty overalls, and almost collided with Paula.

"What do *you* want?" He sounded angry. "Be off with you!"

"We live next door." Now Paula's heart was thumping even harder.

"You'll be the new kid, then. Well, you're not wanted here. This is private property. Didn't you see the notice?"

"No, I didn't, actually," replied Paula."I just thought there might be another way out. You see, I'm a bit nervous of dogs…"

"Dog's chained up," said Mr Dredge, still sounding as unfriendly as could be.

"Yes, I know." Paula was beginning to feel scared. The sheds looked threatening, and the horrible smell was making her feel sick. And this farmer wasn't at all like the jolly ones in story books. Still, she told herself firmly, there was nothing to worry about. She could be home in about one minute, if she ran all the way.

With this comforting thought in mind, she added boldly, "I just came to bring Mrs Dredge's jug back. I expect you're Mr Dredge?"

"That's me," replied the man. "So, what do they call you, then?"

"Paula."

"Well, Paula, you'd better make yourself scarce. Hop it! We're not keen on kids nosing around. Or anyone else for that matter. On health

"What do you want? Be off with you!"

grounds, see?"

"Yes," said Paula meekly, though she couldn't imagine what Mr Dredge meant. Then, hardly able to believe her own daring, she went on, "I did just wonder…What's in your sheds? I mean, I haven't seen any animals on your farm. None at all."

Suddenly she felt foolish, remembering that not all farmers keep animals. Perhaps Mr Dredge grew potatoes. Or wheat. Perhaps the sheds were full of those things. Absolutely tonnes of the stuff, waiting to be collected!

"Hens," said Mr Dredge.

"Hens?" Paula was puzzled. "*Just* hens?"

"Quarter of a million of 'em." Mr Dredge paused for a moment, then added, "Give or take a few hundred."

"A quarter of a *million* hens?" Paula was astonished. "But where are they all?"

"In the sheds, of course. Where do you think?" The farmer was getting impatient. He had work to do.

"A quarter of a million!" repeated Paula. "But how do they all fit in? Are you quite sure you really mean such a lot?" Again, Paula was surprised at her own boldness, and fearing that at any moment Mr Dredge would lose his temper. But he seemed happy enough to explain.

"Ten sheds, twenty-five thousand per shed. Do your sums, girl. Comes to what I said, give or take."

"But do they actually like it in there?" Paula simply couldn't imagine the scene.

"*Like* it?" said Mr Dredge. "Course they like it. I can tell you, when I leave the shed doors open on a nice summer's day, my hens are in the next best place to heaven. Got everything they could possibly want, and more."

"Really?" said Paula.

"Yes, really. Now, you get on home, like I said." And with that he stomped off, heading for the next shed.

"Please, can I see them? Not all of them, of course. Just some?" Paula called after him. She could be persistent. Her father was inclined to call the quality 'being a nuisance', or 'winding people up'.

Mr Dredge turned and looked at her, his expression dubious. Then he gave a shrug.

"Don't see why not, seeing as you've got your boots on. Clean them in that."

He pointed to a shallow tank of murky liquid by the entrance of shed 10 (every shed had its number roughly painted above the door). Whatever the liquid was, it had a greasy film on it, and reeked of strong disinfectant. Paula dipped one wellie-clad foot in the tank, then the other.

"Follow me," commanded Mr Dredge. "But when we get inside, mind you keep nice and quiet, and move around slowly. I don't want my birds upset. They don't take at all kindly to strangers!"

Chapter 4
Inside shed 10

Mr Dredge led the way into a small annexe, stuffed to the roof with cardboard boxes and egg cartons. The cartons had bright labels on them, printed with a cheerful scene showing a farmhouse set amongst rolling hills, and each one bore the words Folly Farm Eggs from Happy Hens

A thin, dark-haired young man was sitting at a bench in one corner sorting out eggs, but he didn't look up.

"That's Mike," said Mr Dredge, nodding in the direction of the young man. "Now, you just follow me." And he heaved aside a heavy sliding door and went ahead of Paula into the shed.

Paula knew she would never forget the moment when she first saw the rows of cages, stacked from floor to ceiling, several tiers high. And she knew she'd never forget the first time she heard the sound of twenty-five thousand hens, all together in one building.

It took a few seconds for her eyes to become accustomed to the gloom, and to realize that the ghostly impression was due to the myriads of cobwebs that hung from the roof girders, and festooned various iron struts and items of machinery. Dusty light bulbs glowed dully the length of the aisle down which Mr Dredge was leading the way, between hundreds of cages. The air was warm, and thick with the peculiar sickly smell Paula had noticed earlier. Already her throat felt dry and scratchy.

Thousands of birds were eagerly thrusting their heads through the bars of the cages. Some had quite a good covering of feathers, while others appeared to have almost none at all.

"What do you call these kind of hens?" asked Paula, who was trying not to breathe in too much of the smelly air.

"Battery hens, these are," replied Mr Dredge proudly.

"Oh, I see," said Paula in a small voice.

"Got to fix a dodgy cage front. Won't take a minute," said Mr Dredge. "You stay there and be having a look. Remember, though, keep nice and quiet."

And with that he pulled some odd bits of string from his overall pocket and made his way towards the far end of the shed.

Paula stood stock still, staring. She could feel the tears starting to her eyes. Why, there were three, no at least *four* hens in each tiny cage. Most were jostling for space, while those near the front were thrusting their heads and necks through the cage bars, fixing her with beady eyes. One even tried to peck at a bright hair slide she was wearing. Some had damaged beaks, with blunt or jagged ends, and one little hen lay on her side. She might be dying, thought Paula sadly.

"Oh, you poor, poor birds," she whispered, the tears running down her cheeks. "You can't even spread your wings."

Then she forced her eyes to travel upwards, to the highest row of cages. One hen on the topmost tier seemed to be staring down at her, with a particularly intense expression.

"Hello, you poor little battery hen," said Paula, remembering to

18

speak very quietly, though that seemed a strange thing to have to do amid the continuous din made by thousands of birds. "Whatever have they done to you?"

The hen leant further out between the cage bars.

One hen on the topmost tier seemed to be staring down at her

And then a very extraordinary, indeed a most astonishing and amazing thing happened.

The hen spoke.

"Come back on your own, if you can, my friend," the hen said, "and I'll tell you all about it. Yes, only return, and I'll fill you in on every single miserable, rotten, cruel aspect of this dismal place!"

Paula felt dizzy. It must be the heat, she told herself firmly. The heat, combined with this awful smell and the feeling of stress. Yes, that was it. She was simply imagining things. Because hens don't talk!

Her knees were trembling so much that she feared they might buckle under her. "I must get out of here before I faint," she muttered, her heart pounding.

"But come back, I beg of you," said the hen on the top tier, speaking remarkably clearly, and seeming to be able to read Paula's mind. "You see", she went on, "*you* can get out of here, but for us it's a life sentence. That's the difference."

"Who are you?" Paula called up, as soon as she felt she could utter a sound.

"I'm Minny," replied the hen, "and I've been standing or crouching on this wire floor for the best part of a year. Yes, I'm Minny, a proud descendant of the Red Jungle Fowl." Minny put her head on one side and leant out a little further. "Say you'll come back. You see, you are our only hope."

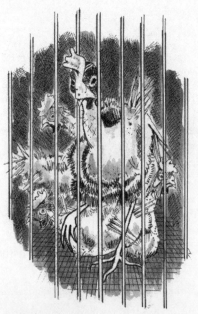

"I'm Minny," replied the hen.

Paula clung onto a dirty cobwebby iron strut for support. Her legs were still shaking, and she felt very strange. She was about to speak, when she saw Mr Dredge advancing towards her through the gloom. Paula realized that if she were ever to find Minny again, she must make a mental note of the exact position of her cage. Top row, fifth cage along, in the centre aisle: that's what she must remember! She knew she'd recognise Minny easily enough by her poor blunt beak and her feathers. Well, by the *absence* of feathers, for Minny had hardly any.

"I'll be back, Minny," Paula called up in a whisper. "You can depend on me." Then quickly she brushed the tears from her cheeks and turned towards Mr Dredge.

"Well, what do you think to my hens?" he enquired, pulling a long strand of cobweb out of his hair. "Not bad little layers, this lot."

"Oh, they're lovely!" Paula was amazed to hear herself lying so convincingly. Nobody had ever thought much of her acting abilities - for school plays she'd usually ended up helping to paint the scenery. "Thank you for showing me round," she added.

"Best be off, now. It's time for the lads' and my coffee break. Ten o'clock sharp's our time. Anyway, your mum will be wondering where you've got to."

"Right, yes, she will! Bye then, and thanks again."

Once she was through the packing annexe and outdoors again Paula broke into a run, taking in great gulps of fresh air. The smell of the battery shed seemed to be trapped in her nose, and clinging to her clothes. As she passed the farmhouse she forced herself to slow down. She must remember to walk calmly past Prince, and at a safe distance. He was chained up as usual, and lying in front of his kennel.

"Hi, Prince," she said gently, thinking that he looked as if he was in need of a friend almost as much as Minny. The dog let out a low growl, but stayed where he was, just following Paula with his amber eyes. With relief, Paula slipped out of the gate and across the lane, and home to Orchard Cottage.

"You've been a long time. I was beginning to wonder," said Paula's mother. "Been chatting to Mrs Dredge?"

Mrs Brown was feeling pleased with herself. She'd been unpacking boxes of kitchen equipment and finding just the right places for her favourite things. Old newspapers, used to pack fragile items, were now strewn over the floor. "I even wondered if you'd found someone to play with. Your dad said he spotted a boy's bike in one of the Dredges' outhouses. About your size," she added.

"I didn't see anyone. Only Mr and Mrs Dredge."

"Oh well, we'll find out soon enough. You could do with someone to make friends with. Nearby, I mean."

"Actually, I did see their chickens. Mr Dredge showed me around."

"There! What did I say? I knew it must be a proper farm, with animals!"

"Oh yes, lots," replied Paula, thoughtfully.

How could she possibly tell her mother about Minny? Who in the whole wide world would believe she'd had a conversation with a hen? And if she described the horrible farm in any detail, her mother might forbid her to go anywhere near it.

No, Minny must remain Paula's secret. Somehow, she must find a way to return to shed 10. Somehow, she absolutely must get to hear Minny's story.

Chapter 5
Minny's ancestors

"Can I join the library?" Paula asked her mother at breakfast the next day.

She was determined to discover as much as she could about Minny. How could that skinny little creature rightfully claim to be something as grand sounding as a direct descendant of the Red Jungle Fowl? Was Minny telling the truth?

 "I've finished the book I was reading," she added.

"That's a good idea," said Mrs Brown. "We could go tomorrow."

"Can't we go today?" pleaded Paula. "*Please,* Mum."

Mrs Brown was surprised. She'd have thought the library would be the last thing on her daughter's mind, with all the excitement of the move. Why, the child had hardly had time to explore the orchard properly. Still, Paula was an unusually keen reader, and Mrs Brown had always been proud of that.

"I suppose we could," she agreed. "There's a bus at half-past two. Apparently it stops outside the Black Horse. Why don't we catch that?"

"Thanks, Mum. I could stay in the library while you go to the supermarket." Already Paula had worked out that she'd need some time alone; time in which to find a book about chickens without her mother asking awkward questions.

"That's not a bad idea. We'll enrol you straight away, then I'll go off and do my shopping while you have a good browse."

By three o'clock Paula had whispered goodbye to her mother in the hushed and softly carpeted library. Without much thought, she selected an adventure story and took it to the librarian's desk.

"Excuse me, but I need to find out about the Red Jungle Fowl," she said, blushing.

The librarian smiled, not seeming to find her request in the least bit odd.

"Sounds as if you've an interesting project on," she said. "The Red Jungle Fowl, you say? That's a kind of chicken, isn't it? The original chicken, I seem to remember. I think I know just the thing." And she crossed the library and took down a heavy reference book from a top shelf.

The volume was large, and on its cover were beautiful coloured photographs showing many different breeds of fowl. The librarian consulted the index.

"Here we are," she said, after what seemed an age to Paula. "It tells you all about the Red Jungle Fowl, right here, at the beginning."

"Thank you. Thank you very much."

Paula took the book and sat down by the window. She started by leafing through the pages, stopping at every illustration. "Well," she thought, puzzled,

"Minny doesn't look remotely like any of these. None of Mr Dredge's chickens does." But regardless of this, Paula decided that Minny's claim had to be properly investigated. Fortunately, the book was written in an interesting way, and soon Paula was deep into the first chapter.

She read how Red Jungle Fowl live in rainforests, where vegetation is thick, and how they roost at night in trees and bushes, to be safely off the ground. And how, despite eight thousand years of domestication by humans, the behaviour of the present-day chicken is identical to that of his or her ancestors.

She read how the female has an absolute need to find a quiet, secluded place in which to lay her eggs; and how, once the clutch of several eggs is complete, she will sit on the nest day and night, only leaving it for a few minutes in every twenty four hours, to find food and water. And how, in the past, all hens would lay only about a dozen eggs each year. (This wouldn't please Mr Dredge, thought Paula, not one little bit! From all those boxes in that packing place, it looks like his hens lay one practically every day.)

She found out how chicks learn from their mothers to choose the right things to eat, and how all Red Jungle Fowl spend most of their day pecking around with their beaks for food, and that when chickens are not allowed to search out their own food (as when kept in battery cages, explained the book's author) they become terribly frustrated, and peck each other's feathers out.

" Do you need any help, dear?" the librarian called over to Paula. "You look a little bit worried."

"Oh no, thank you. I'm doing fine." Paula tried to sound cheerful, though really she was feeling increasingly distressed, on Minny's behalf.

Under a heading DIET, the book listed fruits, seeds, herbs and invertebrates. An example of a favourite food was the minute seeds of the bamboo tree. Paula pictured the dull mealy substance in the troughs in shed 10, and she frowned again.

Then she learned about the birds' exceptionally acute powers of hearing, how they can distinguish between twenty different chicken calls. For a few moments Paula sat staring out of the window, hearing in her mind the never-ending confused cacophony in shed 10. Then she turned to the next page.

There, she discovered that all birds have a strong instinct to keep their feathers in perfect condition, which they fulfil by frequent preening and grooming, and by performing something called a dust bath every day. And

Paula thought about Minny, who had hardly any feathers left now, and wondered how she must feel, unable to do this important job.

She found out how Red Jungle Fowl live in small groups of one cockerel to four of five hens. Then Paula realized with a shock that Minny had probably never so much as *seen* a cockerel, let alone watched one performing his interesting courtship behaviour. According to the book he would waltz around the hen of his choice, dragging one wing on the ground, intent on gaining her approval.

Then she read about the agitated pre-laying pacing that hens carry out, if they can't find a quiet, safe place for a nest, and again thought of Minny and her cage-mates, and all the other thousands of Mr Dredge's hens in their congested cages, hemmed in on all sides by metal bars.

Suddenly, Paula realized that her mother might return at any moment. Half an hour had passed since she'd left for the supermarket. She was about to close the book, when an extraordinary piece of information caught her eye. Quickly, she scanned the paragraph, but, to her great annoyance, she couldn't understand it.

Anxiously, she glanced up and down the High Street. No sign of her mother yet.

Feeling rather foolish, Paula carried the heavy book over to the librarian, who was tapping away on her computer, concentrating hard.

"I'm sorry to interrupt you, but I wonder…" started Paula. The librarian pressed one or two keys, then looked up.

"Yes, dear?"

"There's this bit I don't understand. I wonder if you could quickly take a look at this one paragraph?" Paula pointed to halfway down the page. "You see my mother will be back soon, and we have to hurry away." This wasn't strictly true; the bus wouldn't be leaving for nearly an hour. But Paula felt justified; she couldn't on any account risk a general discussion about her reasons for researching chickens.

"Just let me look." The librarian peered over her spectacles. "I see…" she muttered. "Something about embryonic social interaction…how terribly interesting!"

"Yes," said Paula, bursting with impatience. "But I couldn't quite…"

"Well," said the lady, "it's telling us that chicks, even when they're still in their shells, can talk to each other, and that the parent bird can talk to her chicks even before they hatch out. Well, perhaps not *talk*," she added, laughing, "Chickens don't of course talk, do they? But it means they can indicate certain needs, by making certain sounds. How very extraordinary! Well, I don't know about you, but *I've* certainly learned something today."

Paula knew her mother could appear at any moment, but she didn't want to sound abrupt or rude. She shut the book carefully, before handing it back to the librarian.

"Thank you very much for your help. I'll just take this one book today."

"That's lovely," said the lady, stamping Paula's adventure story. "And I hope your project goes really well."

The librarian was reaching up to put the poultry book back on the top shelf where it belonged, when Paula saw her mother about to turn into the library.

"Here's my mum now," she said, trying to keep the relief out of her voice. "Thanks again."

And she pushed her way through the swing doors, and ran out into the sunshine.

Mrs Brown suggested a cup of tea and a bun, as there was a long wait for the bus and they had no more shopping to do.

Paula was unusually quiet, hardly seeming interested in the array of cakes to choose from in the pretty little café they'd found tucked away up a narrow side street.

"Are you feeling all right, Paula?" asked Mrs Brown, in a concerned voice.

" I'm fine," replied Paula, but Mrs Brown continued to glance at her daughter anxiously.

For the whole of the bumpy bus ride home Paula stared out of the window in silence. She was thinking about Minny, and planning all the questions she needed to put to her. From the book in the library, she now knew that Minny shared every single instinct of her wild ancestor, the Red Jungle Fowl. Every single one!

And if that really was true (and Paula felt it had to be true, because the book had been written by an important sounding professor, who taught at an important-sounding university), then there were no two ways about it.

Minny was living in hell.

Chapter 6
The wicked lie

"I'm going out for a bit, Mum."

It was almost ten o'clock the following morning, the time for Mr Dredge's tea break. Paula reckoned there shouldn't be anyone working in Minny's shed, perhaps for half an hour.

"All right, love. But don't go far, will you? And have your mobile with you. I do like to know where you are." Mrs Brown was still busy unpacking boxes and washing out cupboards. She'd be glad of some time on her own.

"OK. Be back soon," said Paula, and ran off, knowing she mustn't waste a precious moment of Mr Dredge's coffee break.

She felt confident of reaching the last shed unseen as long as she kept to the far side of the farmhouse, well away from the kitchen windows. But first she must get past Prince without raising the alarm. Somehow, she and Prince absolutely had to become friends.

Quietly, Paula unlatched the smaller gate and walked calmly up the farm drive. Prince rose slowly to his feet and slunk towards her, his chain dragging on the ground, a low rumble coming from deep in his throat.

"Prince," Paula whispered. "Here, boy." And standing still, at the point she guessed marked the full extent of his chain, she held out the toast she'd hidden in her pocket at breakfast. The nearer he came, the louder the rumblings grew. Paula began to feel in the grip of her old terror of dogs, but she stood her ground.

Then, as he reached her, the growl faded away and quietly he took

29

the toast and returned with it to a patch of ground near his kennel, settling down to enjoy the unexpected treat, holding it steady between his front paws.

"Good boy, Prince," murmured Paula. "Good, *good* boy." And the great dog gave a feeble wag of his tail.

With a pounding heart Paula hurried round the side of the farmhouse. She passed two windows and could see into a large living room: nobody in there, to notice a trespasser! A narrow path, overgrown with weeds, ran alongside the far end of the sheds. At every moment Paula was aware of the risk she was taking. What if a worker, or, worse still, Mr Dredge himself should suddenly appear, demanding to know what she was up to? Whatever happens, remember what you've planned to say, she told herself. Just keep calm.

But all was quiet, except for the low humming sound Paula had noticed before. The day was warm and sunny, and she saw to her relief that the door to shed 10's annexe had been left open. Even the big sliding door into the unit wasn't quite closed, and now she could clearly hear the unceasing clamour coming from the thousands of hens.

Boldly, Paula knocked on the door. If nobody answers, she thought, all well and good. And if they do, I'll ask to buy a dozen eggs. The money, shaken that morning out of her piggy bank, jingled reassuringly when she patted the pocket of her jeans. But all was quiet.

Glancing behind her to make sure she hadn't been followed, Paula hurried across the packing room, then squeezed through the gap into shed 10.

Now the noise from the hens was overpowering, and Paula had to fight a mounting fear of being enclosed in this spooky place. She stood for a moment, trying to feel brave. Paula Brown, she told herself sternly, remember why you're here! Just keep calm, and think clearly.

Count the cages.

Find Minny.

There's not a moment to lose.

As soon as her eyes had adjusted to the gloom, Paula walked slowly along, counting the cages at ground level. On reaching the fifth one, she looked upwards to the top tier.

Ah! There was Minny, anxiously thrusting her head between the cage bars. At the sight of Paula the little hen leaned out even further, revealing her long scrawny neck. Paula felt thankful her cage wasn't at the other end of the shed. At least it was near the exit to the outside world; she could make a quick getaway.

"So, you kept your word," Minny called down, unable to suppress the excitement in her voice.

"I said I'd be back," said Paula. "But I'm afraid I can't stay long. You see, it's most important that nobody finds me in here."

"Well, if time is of the essence, I'll be brief," said Minny briskly. "Basically, there's one terrifically important point I'd like to make, now you've been so kind as to turn up. I've been going over it in my mind non-stop, ever since we met." Minny shifted around, attempting to get a comfortable grip with her claws on the wire floor. "In a sense," she went on, "it puts the whole wretched business in a nutshell."

"Go on," urged Paula, dreadfully aware of Mr Dredge's coffee break time dwindling away.

"It's this," replied Minny. "Please, never, *ever*, call me a battery hen."

"Oh!" Paula was taken aback. This seemed an odd request. Surely, there were more urgent matters to discuss. "But you do live in a battery cage, on a battery farm..." she began.

"That's true, most unfortunately," interrupted Minny. "Of course it's true! I *am* in a battery cage, and I *do* live on a battery farm." And now her voice became shrill. "But I am not, repeat *not* a battery hen." Then she added, quite slowly, as if speaking to a very small child, "A hen in a battery cage is not a battery hen. Which is to say, she is not some kind of newly-invented species!" Minny paused, then concluded, "I trust you follow my logic?"

"Yes, yes... I think so." Paula had certainly not expected their conversation to take this philosophical turn.

"Good," said Minny, sounding calmer. "You see, as I think I mentioned yesterday, I, Minny, am a proud descendant of the Red Jungle Fowl."

"I found out quite a lot about your ancestors," said Paula. "I went to the library. I know all about the sort of things they liked." Now rather in awe of Minny, she added humbly, "Surely, though, you've always lived here, haven't you? I mean, if you've never known anything else…"

"Stop!" squawked Minny. "That's what they all say! But it happens to be a downright lie!"

"A downright lie?" echoed Paula.

"Just so, and a wicked one," replied Minny. "You see, they don't understand, or most likely they just won't admit, that we all suffer from this terrible affliction." And here she paused, and a pained look came into her beady eyes. "It takes the form of a dream-like syndrome, beautiful but cruel. Actually," she added, in a more down-to-earth voice, "the proper term for it is 'ancestral memory'."

"Wow!" said Paula. "That sounds really important."

"For us, it's the most important thing in the whole world," agreed Minny, glancing around her at the other hens. Most were poking their heads through the bars; some were quarrelling as they vied with each other for space, while others squatted down hopelessly. One hen in Minny's own cage was lying against the bars in a corner, clearly exhausted.

"Cage Layer Fatigue," explained Minny, pointing her beak in the direction of the collapsed bird. "It gets a good many of us in the end. Flapper will probably not last the day."

"That's so sad. Poor Flapper." Paula peered at her watch. She could only just make out the time, in the dim light; already it was nearly a quarter past ten. "Tell me about ancestral memory," she urged. "But you'll have to be quick. I definitely mustn't be caught in here."

"Well, where to begin? There's so *much* to tell." Minny put her head on one side, thinking hard. "I know! This morning I'll describe my dreams about searching around for my own food."

Paula had noticed the metal troughs that ran the length of the shed in front of every cage; they were all nearly full of a floury substance.

"But surely," she said, "at least you've plenty of food, right near you. You'll never go hungry in here."

"Garbage!" snorted Minny. "Pure garbage. Calculated to keep us alive (well, most of us, though not poor old Flapper, it seems). Formulated to keep us laying eggs… But, from a hen's point of view, absolute garbage!" she finished passionately.

"What would your dream-food be, then?" asked Paula.

"Oh, insects, grains, worms, seeds, that type of article..."

"Tiny bamboo seeds, for instance..."

"You know about that?" gasped Minny, her eyes wide with astonishment.

"Well, only because of the book in the library," explained Paula, modestly.

"Ah yes, the book. Anyway," Minny went on, "to get at these little seeds and grubs and so on I scratch around in any soft bit of earth on this dream-world forest floor, using my powerful legs and feet..." Here her voice trailed off and she looked wistful, then added angrily "In this place, what good would that be? You'd have to be mad to try any such thing on these wire floors."

"Absolutely," agreed Paula.

"As I was saying," continued Minny, "in my dreams I can actually *feel* the soft earth, I actually *know* the sheer satisfaction of kicking it out behind me, as I work away..."

Suddenly Mr Dredge could be heard, shouting instructions to Mike in the packing annexe.

"Minny, I'll have to go," Paula hissed. "But I promise I'll be back."

"Hen's honour?" pleaded Minny, in a low, urgent voice.

"Hen's honour," breathed Paula. "See you, Minny."

And with that Paula hurried to a corner of the shed, pressing herself against a dusty wall so she could hide behind a hefty iron strut. Heart thumping, she stood listening.

A moment later came the grinding sound of the great sliding door being opened wider. Paula peered round the strut and watched as Mr Dredge and Mike made their way down one of the gangways, stopping now and again to glance briefly into a cage. Twice, Mike opened one and pulled out a dead-looking hen, which he dropped onto the floor.

As soon as the two men were half-way down the shed Paula crept out, managing to reach the farm gate unnoticed except by Prince, who thumped his tail in greeting as she hurried by.

*

Paula was just congratulating herself on her clandestine visit to Minny when someone called "Hi!" and from an nearby outhouse a boy appeared, wheeling a bicycle. He had spiky blonde hair and blue-grey eyes.

"You must be the girl who's moved in next door," he said in a friendly voice.

"That's right," said Paula, greatly relieved not to be accused of trespassing. "I'm Paula."

"Hi," said the boy again. "I'm Jamie. It's about time someone my age lived around here. Will you be starting at Highview after Easter?"

"That's right," said Paula, blushing. Why was she repeating herself? She didn't want to seem stupid. This Jamie looked great, despite most likely being a Dredge.

"We can go together, then," said Jamie cheerfully.

"Cool!" Suddenly the prospect of a new school seemed much less alarming. Now she'd at least know *someone* on the first day.

"See you around, then," said Jamie. "Not tomorrow, though. We're all going out for the day to visit my grandma. She lives miles away.

Someone called 'Hi' and from an outhouse, a boy
appeared wheeling a bicycle. He had spiky blonde hair and blue-grey eyes.

Still, see you soon…"

"Yes, see you," Paula called over her shoulder, as she let herself out of the gate and ran across the lane. It felt like she'd found a friend, and right next door, too. The only trouble was, the task of keeping her visits to Minny absolutely secret suddenly seemed even more complicated.

Chapter 7
A lucky break

Mr Brown was enjoying life. He'd discovered a definite talent for selling cars, both new and second-hand, and Uncle Ian was wondering how he'd ever managed without his brother Des in the business; he was even considering changing the name of the garage from Ian Brown Limited to Brown Brothers Limited.

Just now, Paula and her mother were clearing away the breakfast things, while Mr Brown collected his briefcase and car keys.

"Well, Paula?" he asked his daughter. "What's on the agenda today?"

"Oh, nothing special," replied Paula, feeling guilty. Today should be ideal for another meeting with Minny, and that promised to be very special indeed.

"What about the Dredge boy?" suggested Mrs Brown. "Jamie, did you say he's called? Why not ask him round here?"

"He won't be there. He told me they're all going out for the day. To see his grandma." Whatever happened, Paula knew she must be free to carry out her plan. Now it felt like her parents might be about to try to arrange her day. But to her relief Mr Brown was in a hurry to be off to work.

"Well, we've not been here a week yet," he reminded his daughter. "You'll find plenty to do around the cottage, I'm sure." He kissed his wife and Paula, called out "Bye, then. See you about six," then left the cottage, whistling cheerfully.

Paula made her bed and helped her mother find places for a few more of their belongings, whilst glancing at her watch every few minutes.

Just before ten o'clock she looked out of the window. The trees were being tossed about by a cold March wind, but at least it wasn't raining.

"I think I'll go out for a bit." Paula tried to sound casual.

"Good idea, love, but don't be long. I thought we might go into town again, later." My goodness, thought Mrs Brown, Paula's taking to country life like a duck to water. Seems the child can't get enough fresh air. Funny though, how her clothes and even her hair smell a bit musty, these days, despite her being outside so much of the time.

"OK. See you, Mum."

"Those pockets are awfully bulgy," commented Mrs Brown, frowning. "You make sure you empty them, before those jeans go to the wash. And wear a coat – it's none too warm."

"I will. Bye, then." Paula hurried off, fearing her mother might suggest she should turn out her pockets there and then. How ever could she have explained away the two slices of buttered toast?

This time, Prince was obviously pleased to see Paula, accepting his treat with an enthusiastic thump of his tail. Paula kept back the second slice, in case of emergencies.

She'd started to walk casually in the direction of the sheds when she noticed a huge vehicle parked alongside the first shed. It was brilliant white, and all along its side were painted scenes depicting the greenest of green hills, and a picturesque old-fashioned farmhouse. Below this was the slogan *FRESH AS DAWN EGGS*.

Quickly, Paula made sure she was out of sight, hidden behind a clump of bushes that grew beside the path. She'd already decided that if she met Mike, or another worker, she would claim to be looking for Jamie. But she hadn't planned on this. Still, she thought, it should have been pretty obvious that all those thousands of eggs absolutely had to be collected on a daily basis. Mr Dredge certainly couldn't be selling them all himself, so they must be going to a supermarket or something.

By peering round a bush Paula could see two men and Mike carefully loading large boxes into the back of the vehicle. Then the driver drove to the next shed and the same process was repeated, until at last boxes were being brought from the packing annexe belonging to shed 10.

After what felt like an age, Paula was relieved to hear the sound of the lorry's reversing signal, and to see the vehicle slowly backing up to the yard. At long last it turned and drove away, and she could see Mike making his way to the wooden hut where the workers boiled up a kettle in their breaks. She watched until he disappeared inside. Surely, Mike would be out of the way for a good twenty minutes!

But Paula had just reached shed 10 when Mike re-appeared and started walking briskly towards her. She could feel her palms sweating, but somehow managed to sound casual.

"Hi. Is Jamie around?" she called out.

"Jamie? No he's not. Whole family's gone off for the day. Try again tomorrow." And with that Mike got onto a motor bike parked near the hut, pulled a crash helmet over his head, and kicked the engine into life.

"Thanks," called Paula, though she knew he probably wouldn't hear her above the roar of the engine. She stood listening to the splutter of the bike growing fainter, as Mike headed off towards the main road. Now it seemed that not only the Dredges but Mike too would be out of the way, perhaps for several hours.

"Oh Minny, we are in luck," breathed Paula.

Chapter 8
Paula all alone

For a moment Paula hardly dared try the door to the packing annexe. Just suppose it were locked? But to her relief the handle turned easily and she crept in, only to find the room in near-darkness. Paula guessed that the big sliding door into the main unit was at least partially open, for she could see a shaft of feeble light, and clearly hear the unceasing noise made by the hens. But would it be open far enough? It looked too heavy for her to heave any further.

Paula fumbled around, feeling along the wall to where she guessed the light switch would be. Ah! There it was. Now she could see properly, she knew she'd almost certainly be able to squeeze through the gap.

By breathing in and making herself as slim as possible Paula just managed it, emerging on the other side covered in dust and cobwebs.

And now Paula was very, very scared. More scared than she'd ever been in her life.

Whatever was she doing, she wondered, all alone in a huge, horrid, dimly lit place, amid this frightening din? And then the thought came to her that nobody in the whole world knew where she was. *And* she was trespassing.

She'd even forgotten to dip her feet in the filthy old footbath. She'd be in the most terrible trouble if Mr Dredge came back unexpectedly and found her here! Worse still, what if Mike had intended to lock the outer door? What if he returned, to make good his mistake? She'd left her mobile on the kitchen table. She could be trapped in here all day, maybe until tomorrow morning! While all these thoughts were going through Paula's mind, her heart was thumping so hard it seemed to be pulsating in her ears.

But then Paula seemed to hear the words 'hen's honour' inside her head, spoken in Minny's high-pitched voice, and she made up her mind to be brave.

"You're here for a reason, Paula Brown," she reminded herself sternly. "So don't you dare be a coward."

And against the awful sound of the complaint of twenty-five thousand hens, she said, quite loudly, "Hi Minny, I've come to visit you."

And Paula walked quickly over to where she knew she would find Minny.

Chapter 9

Minny's secret dream world

Minny was leaning out as far as she could between the cage bars, gazing down at Paula's upturned face. She looked distraught.

"I thought you'd never come!" she exclaimed. "It's been bedlam here today."

"Oh Minny, whatever's been happening?" asked Paula.

"Well, for a start, Mr Dredge was in here well before we'd all finished laying. Generally, you know, there's a fixed pattern, so at least we know what to expect. But not this morning!"

"I suppose he had to get his jobs done early. The family's gone out for the whole day," explained Paula. "They're visiting Jamie's grandma."

"Good riddance!" squawked Minny, shifting her position uncomfortably.

It was then that Paula noticed Flapper. She was lying completely still on the cage floor, her head at a strange angle.

"Dead," commented Minny, noticing Paula's concern. "She gave up the struggle an hour or so ago. And now old Crosspatch and Goldie are trampling all over her."

"That's dreadful! How long will she be left like that?" asked Paula.

"Oh, until tomorrow. Maybe longer. It depends if anyone spots her. These high cages, and the low ones, they're the worst. It's practically dark at ground level, and we're *really* out of the way up here." Minny fell silent for a moment.

"You were going to tell me more about yourself," Paula reminded her gently.

"And I will," replied Minny, sounding a little calmer. "If you'll promise faithfully not to laugh at me, then I'll allow you a glimpse into my secret dream world. I go there as often as I can," she added quietly.

"Oh *please*," urged Paula, "And of course I won't laugh at you."

"In that case," said Minny resolutely, "here goes." And a faraway look came into her eyes.

"In some ways," Minny began, "it may surprise you to learn that dreaming makes my life more painful. Yet on the other hand, maybe it's dreaming that keeps me going. *Something* does, in this dump. You know, sometimes I find myself wishing that I weren't so terribly strong. Flapper, you see, is right out of it. Really, one can only envy her."

"When do you dream, Minny?" asked Paula softly, bringing her back to the matter in hand.

"A good question," replied Minny. "In fact, there's precious little time off, in this place. But the lights do go out, after seventeen hours or so of all this wretched standing around. I suppose it could be said that we have a sort of night time."

"I'll allow you a precious glimpse into my dream world."

44

"And then?" prompted Paula.

"Well," said Minny, "once we've recovered from the shock of being plunged into darkness, with not so much as a hint of twilight, most of us tuck our heads under our wings and escape from it all for a few hours. Of course, those of us in the old style cages can't even perch. We just have to settle down as best we can, on this beastly sloping wire. And I gather when perches *are* provided they can be most uncomfortable."

Minny paused for a moment, then added wistfully. "The terrible thing about dreaming beautiful dreams is that you have to wake up and face another day."

"So what exactly do you dream *about*?" persisted Paula.

"I'm getting round to that," said Minny, suddenly looking more cheerful. "By far my favourite dream goes something like this. But please don't ask me where the precise images come from, because I've simply no idea."

"Just describe what you see," said Paula impatiently.

"It begins with me waking from a comfortable sleep in a safe roosting place in a tree. Well off the ground, you understand," began Minny. "I jump down, and find myself in a little orchard. It's a most perfect dawn, fresh and lovely, and the apple blossom is so pretty, against a clear blue sky flushed pink by the rising sun. The grass is all damp with dew, and so cool under my feet! Straight away, I start scratching around in some soft earth under a shrub, searching for insects…"

"Just like the Red Jungle Fowl, except this isn't the jungle…" interrupted Paula.

"Exactly," agreed Minny. "Anyway, as I was saying, it's a gorgeous day, and by the time I've rooted around a bit, and had a drink or two of water, the sun's fully up, and I lie for a few minutes with my wings spread out, basking in its warmth."

"How amazing, that you know about these things, even in here," breathed Paula.

"Ancestral memory at work," stated Minny. "I did mention it to you before. Now, shall I go on?"

"Oh *please,*" said Paula, a little afraid that she'd offended Minny.

"Well," continued Minny, "very soon I feel the time is right to lay an egg, so I begin looking round for a safe, secret place for my nest,

45

somewhere among the bushes and tall grasses. All this takes quite a while – you can't rush these things."

"Of course not," agreed Paula, since Minny seemed to be expecting some kind of response.

"Well, eventually I do lay my egg, and I have the satisfaction of sitting on it for a few minutes. (In here, you know, our eggs simply roll away down this vile sloping floor, the moment they're laid.) Then I get up, and start clucking like mad, I feel so glad about the egg." Here Minny paused, looking wistful.

"Go on," urged Paula.

"There's not much more to come," said Minny. "Just a few nice little details. You see, it's turned out to be a perfect, hot day, and in the middle of the afternoon I have a little doze, in the shade of an old plum tree. But basically, and I really must stress this fact, I like to keep busy from dawn till dusk. Hens do, you know. Always on the go. Busy, yet content."

"And in here you've absolutely nothing to do. Nothing at all!" said Paula.

"Too right," said Minny with feeling. "That's the terrible truth. And it's the main reason why so often we pluck each others' feathers out." And here Minny lowered her voice, adding, "Or even end up killing each other."

"Not Flapper…?" whispered Paula. "Surely you didn't…?"

"Oh, not Flapper! No, I told you, Flapper's a victim of Cage Layer Fatigue pure and simple. Actually, she was pretty active on the pecking front herself, until she lost her strength. You'll hardly have failed to notice that I've precious few feathers to my name. Well, I can thank old Flapper for that!"

"Yes, I had sort of noticed," murmured Paula politely.

"Still, you can hardly blame us if we *do* become aggressive. It's the stress! Particularly the stress of laying our eggs in front of each other, with nowhere to hide, no secret places to go to. I'd say that's the worst torture, I really would…Plus the ghastly boredom."

"Do you want to tell me more about your dream world?"

"Another time, I will. Right now, I feel emotionally drained. You see, just re-living my dreams fills me with a quite unbearable longing, a terrible feeling of…" And now Minny seemed too choked to be able to finish her sentence.

"I understand," said Paula. "But do tell me one thing. Why is your beak so... so sort of jagged?"

"Oh that!" scoffed Minny. "Well, the theory goes that if you cut off the sharp end of our beaks, we'll not be able to peck each other to death."

"What a dreadful idea!" gasped Paula.

"Stupid, too," said Minny. "Half the time it doesn't even work. Beaks can re-grow, like Flapper's did. Not mine though. They did a thorough job on mine. As you can see, it's a sorry sight."

"The theory is, if you cut the sharp end of our
beaks, we'll not be able to peck each other to death."

"Did it hurt? When they cut the end off?"

"*Hurt*? I'll say it did," replied Minny, her voice shrill. "The trouble is, it still hurts, even after all this time." She looked thoughtful for a moment, then added, "I'd describe it as a dull ache."

"But that's awful," exclaimed Paula.

"Awful and shaming," agreed Minny. "You see, even when I had my feathers, I no longer felt inclined to groom them. Quite often, I'd skip the task,

47

just because of the ache. But I do so hate looking shabby."

And now Paula didn't want to hear any more. Not today. Minny's story was far sadder than she'd imagined.

Then a quite brilliant idea came to her.

"Minny," she said, with new energy in her voice, "Don't give up hope. Please don't!"

Minny leaned out of her cage as far as she could. "Not give up hope!" she echoed. "Can you kindly give me one good reason for hope, in this prison?"

"I'm going to buy you!" Paula told her. "And I'm going to take you home with me. Won't that be great?"

"Oh, truly great!" agreed Minny, "But goodness only knows how you'll manage to pull that one off. It sounds a most ambitious plan. And, to be quite honest, rather too good to be true."

"I'll do my very best," said Paula. "Hen's honour I will! But Minny, just promise me one thing. Promise me you'll keep well. Don't give up hope, like poor Flapper."

"I'll do my utmost not to," replied Minny, barely able to repress the excitement in her voice. "Hen's honour I will!"

Then Paula said goodbye to Minny and squeezed through the gap in the big sliding door, not forgetting to switch off the light in the packing annexe on her way out.

Chapter 10
The catchers are coming

"Hi, Mum! I'm back."

Mrs Brown was in the living room, arranging her collection of china dogs on a shelf next to the fireplace. The cottage was really beginning to look like home.

"Hello, love. My goodness, you look a bit dusty. Wherever have you been?"

Paula brushed a cobweb from her sleeve. "Oh, just round and about."

Mrs Brown wrinkled her nose. "And there's that peculiar smell again. I noticed it yesterday, too."

"Mum. Please can I keep a chicken? Or two or three, perhaps." Paula felt a quick change of subject was needed, to distract her mother from the subject of smells.

"Chickens! Goodness, I don't know, Paula."

"Please, Mum. I do want some."

"But wouldn't chickens be a lot of trouble? And it seems a bit silly, when we can get fresh eggs right next door." Mrs Brown didn't know a thing about chickens, and could well imagine herself having to…well, she wasn't sure what exactly, but they were bound to need plenty of attention.

"I'll look after them. Feed them and clean them out and everything," insisted Paula.

"Well, maybe. Just *maybe*, mind. You'll have to ask your dad. He'd be the one having to make an enclosure, or whatever. We couldn't just let them run wild."

"Tonight, then. I'll ask him when he gets home."

"Not till he's had his tea, though," warned Mrs Brown. "You know what he's like, when he gets back tired and hungry."

But even after his favourite tea Mr Brown didn't approve of the idea. Not one little bit.

"For heaven's sake, Paula," he said, speaking rather loudly. "We've more than enough to think about, without chickens. There's your room to decorate, *plus* the rest of the cottage, then this huge garden to lick into shape…"

"OK Dad, it was just an idea," muttered Paula.

"Maybe next year," said her mother, and her father grunted in a non-committal kind of way.

But next year will be too late for Minny, thought Paula. She'll never survive another whole year in that place. Not possibly!

"I'm going out for a bit," she said, trying to keep the tears out of her voice.

"Just in the garden, then. It's getting late," said her mother.

"OK," promised Paula, and went to fetch her coat.

A full moon shone over the wild garden, casting deep shadows, while the frosted grasses of the overgrown lawn reflected its cold light. Paula stood gazing at the sky, watching banks of silver-edged clouds as they raced across the moon. Poor Minny, she thought, she's never seen the sun, let alone the moon. And she never will, unless somehow I manage to rescue her.

Just then a car slowed down in the lane and Paula heard a door slam, then the clank of the farm's five bar gate being opened. The Dredges were back. Prince started barking furiously, until Mr Dredge shouted to him to be quiet. Paula could see Mr and Mrs Dredge going indoors, then lights started coming on here and there in the farmhouse.

But Jamie hadn't followed them, and he'd just finished fastening the gate when he looked up and saw Paula.

"Hi," he called.

"Hi," Paula called back.

"Come on over."

"I can't. I've got to stay in the garden. You can come here, though, if you like."

"OK." Jamie climbed over the gate and sauntered across the lane to join Paula.

"How was your grandma?" asked Paula.

"Fine," said Jamie.

"That's good," said Paula. There was a short silence. Then, not knowing what else to say, she added, "We could go indoors if you like. It's quite cold.."

"Let's stay here," said Jamie. "It feels nice outside, after getting all hot in my grandma's house and then the car. Feels like I've been sort of cooped up the whole day."

Suddenly Paula felt absolutely furious, then shocked as she heard her own angry voice.

"What about all your hens, then? How do you think *they* feel? They're cooped up for ever and ever." She wanted to keep calm, but her voice shook, and she thought she might start crying.

"Don't blame *me*." Now Jamie sounded upset too. "They're my dad's hens, not mine. I wouldn't keep them like that, no fear!"

"Can't you talk to him?" Paula pleaded.

"I've tried all that. He won't listen. He just gets furious. So does Mum."

"Well, I think it's horrible," Paula said feebly. There was no point blaming Jamie.

An awkward pause followed, then Jamie said miserably, "Still, they'll be out of it soon. They're going tomorrow. Some of them, anyway." He hunched his shoulders, frowning.

"Going?" said Paula, puzzled. "Going where?"

"To slaughter, of course. That's the only place they ever go. Just the old ones, of course, the ones in the last two sheds."

"The last two? What, sheds nine and ten?"

"What's so special about those ?"

"Oh nothing. I just didn't think the hens in there were all that old, that's all." Paula was glad it was dark. She could feel herself blushing.

"Well, a year and a half's sort of considered old for a battery hen. It's not really, though. My friend Andrew's got a hen who's almost seven."

"So why *will* they be going to…" Paula couldn't bring herself to mention the word slaughter.

"Dad says they've done their best laying by that age. Plus, they're worn out."

"Cage Layer Fatigue, p'raps," suggested Paula.

"Could be, I suppose," agreed Jamie. Then he gave Paula an odd look. For a townie, this kid from next door seemed to know an awful lot about hens. "Anyway, the catchers'll be here in the night. Tomorrow night, that is."

"Catchers? What catchers?" Paula was beginning to feel a mounting sense of dread.

"They come in these huge wagons, about two or three o'clock at night, to catch the birds. You know, they get them out of the cages and sort of chuck them into crates." Jamie paused, then added, "I hope you won't hear it, from your place."

"Hear it? Hear what?" asked Paula anxiously.

"The screams. They sort of scream," said Jamie, scuffing the ground with his trainers.

"Scream? Hens don't scream!" Paula paused, then added, in a whisper, "Do they?"

"Well, not normally, I suppose. Just when they're being caught. It's their bones. They get brittle, in the cages. Plus, I s'pose they must be scared stiff..." Jamie decided not to go on. Most likely this pretty girl wouldn't want to talk to him ever again, if he said much more.

By now Paula's mind was spinning. Tomorrow! The catchers were coming tomorrow night! Somehow, before then, she simply had to rescue Minny. It was unthinkable that Minny should end up on one of those wagons! But first she had to talk her parents into changing their minds.

Just then Paula heard her mother calling her. She turned to Jamie.

"That's my mum. I'd better go. See you, then."

"Yeah, see you around. And I'm sorry about...You know..."

"That's OK. it's not your fault. P'raps see you tomorrow, then."

And with that Paula ran indoors.

"Mum, *couldn't* you persuade Dad about the hens? I'd only want about three."

It was half-past nine and Paula was getting into bed, while her mother pottered around the bedroom, sorting out clothes for the wash.

"I don't think it's quite the moment, love. Maybe next year," said Mrs Brown.

"But it's important, Mum. *Really* important," Paula insisted. "Please, Mum."

"Well, it so happens there are *more* important things, Paula, so you'll have to wait and see. You can't always have what you want, just when you want it." Mrs Brown was beginning to feel distinctly impatient with her daughter. "So, let's change the subject, shall we? I was about to tell you that your dad had a phone call from Grandpa Brown, just a few minutes ago. It seems poor Grandma's had a fall."

"A fall?"

"I'm afraid so. Luckily, it's Sunday tomorrow, so there's no problem with Dad getting time off. We can all go over there for the day, and see how Grandma really is. Grandpa wasn't too clear, on the phone. He was all upset."

"Poor Grandma! Will she be all right?" Paula asked anxiously. She was extremely fond of Grandma Brown.

"Oh, I think so," replied her mother. "She's pretty shaken up, though. Seems she took a tumble down that step in the hall. The doctor says it's just bruising. But at her age…We must go over and see for ourselves how she is."

Then Paula remembered. Tomorrow was Minny's last chance!

"Do we absolutely have to go *tomorrow*?"

"Well of course we must," snapped Mrs Brown. "We're not going to wait, are we? It's *now* she needs us."

"I know, but…"

"No 'buts'," said Mrs Brown briskly, wondering what on earth had got into her daughter. "Now, you try and get off to sleep. I must say, you look a bit peaky for a girl who spends half her time outdoors." She switched off the light, saying in a gentler voice, "Night night, love, and don't you worry about Grandma."

As she bent to kiss Paula Mrs Brown wondered again about that strange, musty smell. Goodness, she thought, she'd make jolly sure Paula had a bath and a hair wash first thing tomorrow. *And* a complete change of clothes.

Chapter 11
The Dredges At War

"Paula, love, just nip next door, will you?" said Mrs Brown. "We'll need an easy snack when we get back from seeing Grandma, and I'm right out of eggs. The money's on the table." She was busy making a large pile of sandwiches, determined to be no trouble to Grandma and Grandpa Brown; they had enough to worry about. "We're planning to leave in half an hour, so hurry back."

"Fine." Paula sounded dejected.

Mrs Brown turned to her daughter. "And do cheer up. I'm sure Grandma will be all right, and she'll be so pleased to see us, and especially you."

"I know." Paula was finding it hard to think about anything except the catchers arriving in the dead of night to yank Minny out of her cage by her poor weak legs. "I'll be quick."

This time she had nothing for Prince, but even so he thumped his tail when she skirted round his kennel. His blanket looked dirty and damp. Poor old Prince, Paula thought, it's not fair, keeping him outside all the time.

As she approached the farmhouse Paula could hear raised voices, and saw that the kitchen door was open; it sounded like Mr and Mrs Dredge and Jamie were quarrelling bitterly. She paused, and stood where she couldn't be seen; it would be awkward to walk straight in on a family row.

"There's no way I'm spending a fortune on that lot, not at this stage. The whole flock will be gone this time tomorrow," Mr Dredge shouted.

"But Dad, you said it went wrong *last night*. That'll mean more than

55

twenty-four hours without water!"

"Well, they'll not be needing it the same, with no food to wash down. The troughs are nearly empty, remember?"

"Dad..." Now Jamie was shouting too.

"Don't you dare yell at your father like that." It was Mrs Dredge's turn. "Of course he can't get anyone in, just for that. Plumbers charge the earth, and this whole place has been losing money for years." She paused, adding wearily, "Anyway, the equipment won't be used again, so what's the point?"

"Why won't it be used again?" Jamie turned to his father defiantly.

"You mind your own business why not, lad. Them hens is only worth a few pence each, if that. In fact, they're rubbish. Now, for Pete's sake go and find yourself something useful to do." And with that he stomped out of the farmhouse, making off in the direction of the sheds, not noticing Paula, as she stood half-hidden behind a holly bush.

"What did he mean, Mum?" Jamie persisted. "Why won't the equipment be used again?"

"Like your Dad says, it's no concern of yours. Now, are you going to wash my car and earn yourself some pocket money, or are you not?"

"OK," said Jamie sullenly.

"Get on with it, then," said his mother, "I'll be needing it this afternoon. I've got a hair appointment. Now, for God's sake leave me to sort these bills out."

Jamie appeared outside, head down, hands deep in the pockets of his jeans. It was a moment before he saw Paula standing there.

"Oh, hi!" Jamie's face brightened.

"Hi. Mum sent me to buy some eggs. But perhaps it's not a good moment. I didn't like to..." Paula didn't quite know what to say. Perhaps she shouldn't let Jamie know she'd heard all the shouting.

"It's OK. There's millions in the kitchen. Just knock first, though. My mum's in a foul mood." Jamie looked upset. "The water's not getting through in shed 10. The pipe's blocked somewhere. Dad thinks the hens will be OK till... You know, till they go. *I* don't think they will." His voice tightened in anger.

"Oh, the poor things." Paula was imagining Minny, desperately thirsty on top of all her troubles. "Can't you do anything?"

"No I can't," replied Jamie. "What *can* I do? They won't listen to me. I'm just a kid."

"I know," said Paula sadly. "Anyway, I'll have to go now. We're visiting my grandma and grandpa for the day."

"And I've got to wash Mum's car. See you," Jamie said.

Paula stood by the holly bush, plucking up courage to go into the farmhouse. After a moment Jamie emerged from an outhouse, carrying a bucket and sponge.

"See you then, Jamie," said Paula.

Then Paula took a deep breath and knocked on the kitchen door, and a minute later was picking up a box of Folly Farm Eggs from Happy Hens and handing the money to a furious-looking Mrs Dredge.

"Thank you very much," said Paula as she left the kitchen, but Mrs Dredge was concentrating once more on the untidy mass of papers spread out on the table and didn't bother to reply.

If Paula hadn't been so worried about Minny she would have enjoyed the visit to Grandma and Grandpa Brown. Grandma was much better by the time they arrived, and their little house felt its usual bright, cosy self. But Paula couldn't get Minny and the catchers out of her mind.

"Is something the matter?" Grandpa Brown asked Paula kindly when they were on their own, looking at some frog-spawn in the pond. "You can tell me, you know."

But she couldn't, and that was the trouble. It seemed the only person she could share her worries with was Jamie, and there was no way he could help.

For the whole of the journey home Paula was unusually quiet. She was thinking hard. There just had to be a solution!

By the time the Browns arrived back at Orchard Cottage Paula had come up with a plan. It was a daring one, and merely thinking about what it involved made her heart beat faster.

She had resolved that tonight she would save Minny, however great the risks.

Chapter 12
The midnight adventure

At bedtime, Paula set her alarm clock for midnight and hid it under her pillow. But she was so worried in case its muffled ring should fail to wake her that she couldn't fall asleep. Instead, she lay staring at the square of moonlight on the wall opposite her bed, her mind racing.

Paula had never gone against her parents' wishes in anything really important. She'd never crossed a forbidden road, or stolen sweets from the corner shop near the flat, like some kids did. But here she was, planning to creep out of the cottage at midnight, to steal three hens! No, not *steal*, she reminded herself. She'd taken all the money out of her piggy bank and carefully sealed it up in an envelope, addressed to Mr Dredge. She would leave it in Minny's empty cage. Surely what she planned to do couldn't count as stealing?

As the hours to midnight ticked slowly by, Paula tried to think herself into feeling brave. But really she was very scared. Because, one way or another, she knew she was heading for big trouble.

At long last the alarm clock went off, whirring angrily under the pillow. Paula silenced it quickly and got out of bed. She'd left warm socks, jeans and a thick fleece at the end of the bed and she pulled these over her pyjamas, before ramming a woolly hat over her tousled hair. Then she picked up a torch from the bedside table.

Bright moonlight lit the landing. As Paula crept past her parents' room she could hear her mother's steady breathing and her father's faint snore. A board creaked loudly, and Paula stopped for a moment, her heart thudding, but no-one stirred.

Now she went stealthily down the staircase and unlatched the door at the bottom of the stairs that led into the kitchen. There was no need to switch a light on, for moonlight was streaming through the un-curtained windows. For a few seconds Paula leant up against the range, enjoying its comforting warmth.

She was feeling sick. The prospect of her parents' anger was upsetting enough, but thinking about Mr Dredge's reaction was frightening. Perhaps she would be sent away, to wherever they put children instead of prison. Perhaps...

Paula wrenched her hat off and stood staring into space. There was no need for all this! She could simply go back to bed! Nobody in the whole world need ever know about her crazy scheme. It could remain a secret, never to be told.

But then she pictured Minny, crouching asleep at this very moment on the wire floor of her cage, pressed up against Goldie and Crosspatch and maybe Flapper too, dreaming her impossible dreams.

She imagined the catchers, trundling along in their huge wagons, drawing ever closer to Folly Farm.

She thought about the birds' shock when the lights went on and sheds nine and ten suddenly filled with loud voices, as the catchers started on their task. And she felt the terror of the little creatures as they were dragged from their cages and thrust into crates, to be driven miles through the frosty night, many with hardly a feather to keep them warm.

Then, inside her head, she heard Minny's voice saying "Hen's honour", and her own voice repeating the words.

Paula took a deep breath, pulled her hat firmly back on, and left the warmth of the kitchen.

How could she possibly let Minny down?

Paula groped around in the lobby by the back door. Behind a clutter of cardboard boxes, she'd hidden a wicker cat basket, a lucky find she'd made in the garden shed earlier that day. Inside was the envelope addressed to Mr Dredge, containing all the money she'd managed to save towards a new skateboard. Surely that would be enough? Paula picked the basket up, then stepped into her cold wellies and quietly let herself out of the cottage.

It was a cold, clear night, with no need for a torch; brilliant moonlight cast black shadows of trees and hedges across a silvery world. An owl hooted in the wood above Orchard Cottage, and a tiny moonlit creature scurried into the long grasses beside the path, just in front of Paula.

Soundlessly, Paula unlatched the garden gate and stepped into the lane.

And now she knew there was no going back. Somehow, she must succeed in her mission to rescue Minny. For, as Minny had said, Paula truly was her only hope.

Chapter 13
Out of reach!

Paula's carefully laid plans included a treat for Prince – this time a large chunk of left-over pizza crust she'd retrieved from the kitchen bin.

"Prince, here boy, good Prince," she whispered, and the dog stole towards her and took the offering, hardly able to believe his luck.

Now Paula started off along the dismal path that ran past the back of the farmhouse and alongside the ends of the ten sheds. She'd only crept as far as the second shed when Prince began to bark frantically. Paula stopped and listened. Now she too could hear a distant rumble, a sound that was growing steadily louder.

Suddenly two powerful headlights, like great eyes, beamed through the darkness and a tall vehicle loomed over the brow of the hill, followed closely by an identical one. The catchers' wagons!

Lights went on downstairs in the farmhouse, and Paula heard the kitchen door opening, following by footsteps thudding across the frosty tarmac and then Mr Dredge's gruff voice, ordering Prince to be quiet. And now came the clanking of the five-bar gate as it was thrown open to admit the wagons which a moment later were turning into the yard, shuddering to a halt in front of the farmhouse.

Paula's heart was racing. The catchers had arrived early! Surely, Jamie had suggested two, or even three o'clock in the morning. Certainly not midnight! She broke into a run, the basket banging against her leg, the cold night air making her gasp for breath. Reaching shed 10 she tried the door to the annexe. Thankfully it was unlocked, and Paula went quickly inside.

For the first time that night Paula used her torch and saw to her relief that the big sliding door into the unit was wide open. Clearly Mr Dredge had everything prepared in readiness for the night's work.

It was eerily silent inside the battery. Paula's torch could only feebly penetrate the total blackness, but in the nearest cages she could just make out the forms of sleeping hens. Some shifted and muttered uneasily as she passed.

She was creeping along to where she estimated Minny's cage to be, and realizing how much harder it was to count the cages by torchlight, when a terrible thought struck her. Minny was on the uppermost tier! Paula couldn't possibly reach up so high to open the cage. She'd never be able to rescue Minny!

All her careful planning was utterly pathetic. Paula had forgotten the one thing that mattered most.

Paula could hear the rumble of the catchers' wagons starting up again, and she realized they were being re-positioned, to park as near as possible to sheds nine and ten.

She shone her torch into a corner where she hoped she could hide, and hurried there, pressing herself against the wall. Seconds later, the lights came on, revealing the dingy banks of cages, the festoons of cobwebs, and the thousands of hens, all waking in shock at the sudden commotion.

"You'll be starting at the far end, as usual?" It was Mr Dredge's voice.

"Right, Guv," replied a tall, rough looking man, who even now was making his way between the cages, down the central gangway. "Me and Wayne'll do this lot. The others can be doing the far side."

"You'll likely find a good few deads. Water supply's been playing up." Mr Dredge was needing to shout now, to make himself heard above the mutterings of twenty-five thousand waking hens. "Just leave them, or drop 'em on the floor. Me and Mike'll sort things out in the morning."

"Will do," promised the rough looking man, disappearing into the far reaches of shed 10.

And then the catching began.

*

Paula stood well back in the shadows. In horror, she listened to the clank of the cage fronts being opened, and heard the screams of the hens. Repeatedly, the tall man and Wayne rushed towards the exit, clutching several struggling hens in each hand, holding them by the legs, upside down. Paula reckoned that every time they passed by they were carrying twenty between them. Then, having stuffed those into crates, they returned, almost running, for the next lot of hens.

Time after time the process was repeated, the terrified hens protesting and flapping their wings in a futile bid to escape.

Paula's heart was pounding. How could she hope to save Minny now, with the catchers closing in, and with absolutely no means of reaching her cage?

Chapter 14

A race against time

"Paula, it's me," whispered a voice in Paula's ear.

Turning in alarm she saw Jamie, his face white in the ghostly gloom.

"Jamie!" Paula gasped, "Whatever…?"

"I saw you, from my bedroom window. I couldn't sleep either, and I looked out and saw you. What do you think you're up to?"

"Oh Jamie, I know it's your dad's place and everything, but I've *got* to rescue Minny…" Paula stopped short. Jamie would think her crazy, naming a hen in amongst all these thousands. "I meant," she went on, "rescue some hens. Well, three actually. I really must have them, Jamie."

"Three?" whispered Jamie. "What do you mean, three?"

"It's just… When your dad showed me round, I sort of took a liking to a particular one. Oh Jamie," Paula was sobbing now, "I must get her out of here, but I can't reach the cage. She's on the top row!"

Jamie was silent for a moment, frowning. Then an idea came to him, though he wasn't at all sure it was a good one.

"There's this trolley thing," he breathed. "Dad got it, 'cause he's meant to try and see into all the cages. He doesn't use it much, but I know where he keeps it. It's over in that corner."

"Can you get it? Without being spotted?" pleaded Paula. "The ones I want are on the right side, in the middle bit. I know exactly where, and the men haven't got there yet."

"I can try," Jamie replied, and he moved stealthily away, keeping as far as possible in the deepest shadows.

With the shed lights on, Paula could now see quite clearly. As soon as the tall man and Wayne were safely out of the way she crept quickly to the central gangway, and stood below Minny's cage.

"Minny, we're coming to rescue you," Paula called, standing on tiptoe and peering upwards. Thank goodness! Minny was still alive. Paula could see her, head and neck extended as far as possible between the cage bars, eyes wild with fear.

"So, you've come at last!" Minny's voice was cracked. "I've never been so terrified in all my life. This is the end, I said to myself when I heard all this ghastly racket." Then she added, in a voice that was scarcely audible, "And the most bitter of ends, it would seem."

"Please don't worry, little Minny." Paula's heart was thudding. Suppose she were to fail her special hen? Just suppose she had to stand by and watch the catchers dragging Minny out by a leg, and Goldie and Crosspatch too. "Just try not to worry," she repeated desperately.

Swiftly, the catchers were working their way towards the near ends of the outer gangways. In just a few minutes they would have cleared all those cages, and be ready to start on Minny's section.

At that moment Paula heard a low rumble. Jamie was hurrying towards her, pushing a tall trolley composed of a ladder with a small platform on top.

"Sorry I've been such ages," he gasped. "I didn't realize the stupid thing had a brake. 'Course it wouldn't move, not with the brake on."

Paula could see that if one of them could stand on the platform it would be easy enough to reach Minny and her cagemates.

Jamie's face was set and anxious.

"We'll have to be quick about it," he said breathlessly, "they're getting closer every second."

Minny was still alive.

68

Chapter 15
The rescue

Jamie stationed the trolley level with Minny's cage and pressed the brake down.

"Who's going to get them out?" he hissed in Paula's ear.

"I will," said Paula. "You just pass me the basket." And with trembling legs she climbed the steps, and Jamie handed her up the basket.

"There's something in it," he called, over the ceaseless noise of distressed hens.

"It's money. To pay for the hens," Paula called down. She removed the envelope and put it on the platform.

"Some catcher will get a surprise!" said Jamie, but Paula wasn't listening. Carefully, she was opening the front of Minny's cage.

"Now, Minny, you first, my little one," said Paula gently. "Just let me get a good grip, right round your wings. Whatever happens, I mustn't drop you."

"Please *don't*. That would be the final insult," agreed Minny, looking down fearfully at the concrete floor far below.

Somehow, Paula managed to get her hands safely around Minny's almost featherless body. The little hen's skin felt prickly and dry, and surprisingly warm.

"Good girl," breathed Paula, easing Minny into the basket. "You stay quietly there, while I get the others."

But removing Goldie and Crosspatch proved a much harder task. They were scared of Paula, and seemed not to understand that she was helping them. Goldie flapped her wings wildly, striking Paula's face painfully with her spiky, ragged feathers. At last Paula was able to hold both wings still, and with relief she thrust the protesting bird into the basket, quickly closing it. She could well imagine Goldie making a bid to escape.

"Do hurry," urged Jamie, from half-way up the trolley steps. "They're nearly ready to start on this lot."

Then Paula was overcome by total panic. For there was no way a third hen would fit into the basket without risking squashing, and perhaps injuring, all three.

"Jamie, you'll have to hold the last one. She'll never fit in the basket."

Desperately, Paula reached into the back of the cage and grabbed Crosspatch, easily enclosing her wings with her two hands. At least, she thought grimly, I'm getting good at this catching business!

Crosspatch was well feathered and seemed very strong. Aware that it was too late to think about being gentle, Paula held on to her tightly, before handing her down to Jamie, who tucked the hen under one arm, then jumped down from the ladder, before re-arranging the squawking bird.

"Hurry!" called Jamie again. He was sounding desperate now. "My dad'll *kill* me if he finds me in here!"

"Coming," said Paula, flinging the envelope containing her savings into the empty cage. Then she backed carefully down the ladder, holding on tightly to the basket. It felt terribly heavy, considering how scraggy both the hens were, especially Minny.

Jamie knew for sure that the catchers had finished emptying all the cages on either side of the outer gangways, so he led Paula to the same dark corner where she'd hidden earlier.

Just then, the tall man appeared, ready to catch the hens from Minny's bank of cages.

"What the hell was that?" he said, pointing to where Paula and Jamie were. "Something moved!"

"Rats, most likely," said Wayne.

"Way too big for a rat," said the tall one.

"Probably the Guv's dog, then," said Wayne, shrugging. "Come on, let's get this lot on the wagon. There's still Hanging Stone Farm to do tonight. The quicker we're out of here, the sooner we'll be clocking off."

"Right," agreed the tall one.

*Somehow, Paula managed to get her hands safely
around Minny's almost featherless body.*

At the outside door he signalled to the other catchers, who were taking a break on the tailboard of the first wagon, now stacked high with plastic crates full to bursting with hens silenced by fear, and the shock of the cold, frosty air.

"Move it, lads," he yelled. "I want us away from here in half an hour flat."

And the catching gang went back into shed number 10, to complete the night's work.

Chapter 16
Before The Storm

Paula and Jamie carried the hens past the sheds, keeping in the inky black shadows cast by a bright moon. They both felt shaky, and their hearts refused to stop pounding. Between them, they'd achieved Paula's aim: they had saved three hens. But now it felt like their worries had only just begun.

Paula's parents were bound to be furious; they would certainly regard what she had done as theft. And Jamie – well, Jamie felt quite sick, imagining his father's reaction if he discovered his own son had helped the townies' kid from next door make off with three live hens!

"You needn't be involved, Jamie," Paula promised, seeming to read Jamie's thoughts. "This was all my idea. Nobody's seen you. You just keep right out of it."

"I don't know," said Jamie, "I didn't have to help you, did I? It was my decision." But he couldn't help feeling hugely relieved that Paula was willing to face his parents' anger alone.

The two were silent for a moment, then Jamie spoke.

"What do we do with them now?"

He was still clutching Crosspatch to his chest. She had calmed down, and was looking around her in astonishment at this interesting moonlit world.

"I'll put them in the kitchen for the night, near the range, so they'll be warm," said Paula. "Crosspatch will have to be on her own, and the others can stay in the basket."

"You've thought up names for them amazingly quickly," said Jamie, amused.

"Oh well, I'm…I'm good at that sort of thing…" stammered Paula.

"Anyway," Jamie went on, "what about tomorrow?" He was picturing Mr and Mrs Brown coming down in the morning, to find three hens in front of their kitchen range. It didn't bear thinking of.

"Tomorrow?" Paula sounded vague. "I haven't quite worked tomorrow out."

They had crossed the lane now, and Paula unlatched the gate into the Browns' garden. "You'd better go home right now, or your dad might lock you out." Suddenly she leant forward and kissed Jamie quickly on the cheek. "You've been brill, Jamie. Thanks a million, zillion times!"

Jamie was glad it was dark. He felt pretty certain that blushes didn't show by moonlight.

"I'll just bring this one into your kitchen. I can be back in bed in one minute flat. The wagons are still there, so I'm OK for a bit. Dad has to wait up till the catchers have gone."

"Right, thanks," said Paula. Then she laughed. "Sorry, I'd almost forgotten you were holding Crosspatch."

Cautiously, Paula opened the back door and the two tiptoed through the lobby and into the kitchen.

"Look, there's still lots of empty boxes from our move," said Paula, shining her torch into a corner. "This one's got newspaper in the bottom."

Paula put the deep box on the floor near the range and Jamie lowered Crosspatch carefully into it. The hen gave a low cluck, and sank down.

"I'll go now, then. Don't forget to give them all a drink. They'll be mega-thirsty, thanks to Dad."

And now Paula was on her own, and very, very worried. All at once she realized she knew nothing about hens, but had three of them, entirely dependent on her. All she did know was that her parents were going to be furious in the morning, and that at this moment, despite suddenly feeling desperately tired, she must look around for something suitable to hold the hens' water.

One box of odds and ends was still waiting to be unpacked, and, right at the bottom, Paula found two small containers. She filled them from the tap in the sink and placed one in front of Crosspatch in her box. Then she knelt down and unfastened the basket.

"Here you are, you two. I know you're thirsty."

"Thirsty?" exclaimed Minny. "You could call that the understatement of the year!"

Straightaway, she dipped her beak deep into the dish, then, raising her head, tipped the cool water down her throat with an expression of rapture.

After that, she and Goldie took turns, until almost all the water was gone. When Paula guessed they'd both had their fill, she took the dish away and secured the door of the basket.

"Excuse *me*!" Minny poked her head out of the wire mesh of the door and glared at Paula. "It occurs to me that this set-up is little better than a battery cage." She paused, before adding, in a milder tone, "Though I do have to admit that the flooring is a great deal more comfortable."

"Oh Minny!" Paula laughed, "it's only for tonight. Tomorrow I'll arrange a nice big corner in the garage for you all, and fill it with straw. Hen's honour I will!"

"Hen's honour?" persisted Minny, sounding a little calmer.

"Absolutely hen's honour," promised Paula. "Now, you just settle down by our nice warm range for what's left of the night, and dream. Believe me, Minny, your dreams are about to come true."

Paula had started to creep out of the kitchen when Minny called her back. Once again, Paula knelt down beside the basket.

"There's just one more point I'd like to clear up, if at all possible," Minny said, in a small, almost tearful voice.

"Yes, Minny?"

"It's simply this. There's *no way*, is there, that anyone could ever again call me a battery hen?" Minny paused, then repeated, in an even smaller voice. "Is there?"

Seeing the little scrap of a hen, with her pink featherless body, stubby tail and damaged beak, Paula's eyes filled with tears. Poking her finger through the mesh of the basket, she gently stroked Minny's rough head.

And then she told a very big white lie.

"Goodness no, Minny," Paula said. "From now on, everyone will know at a glance that you're a proud descendant of the Red Jungle Fowl."

And with this reassurance ringing in her ears, Minny tucked her head under one wing and settled down to sleep.

Paula turned off her torch and left the room, closing the door gently. Silently, she crept upstairs, past her sleeping parents, and into her own room, where she undressed quickly.

Whatever tomorrow held, by way of her parents' shock and the Dredges' fury, Paula knew she had done the right thing. For Minny, Goldie and Crosspatch were safe.

Once back in bed, Paula tried to imagine how her little flock would feel the next day, experiencing a first taste of freedom. How would the hens behave, after a whole year in captivity? Would they want to explore, or might they be too frightened? Would they even know how to walk...?

Paula was puzzling over these things, and still had many more questions in her mind, but in a very few minutes she had drifted into a deep, deep sleep.

Chapter 17
Paula In trouble deep

"Paula!" Mrs Brown was standing beside her daughter's bed, a horrified expression on her face.

Paula barely stirred. She was deep into a dream about hens – thousands of them, roaming happily around a vast sunlit orchard.

"Paula!" repeated her mother shrilly, and at last Paula opened her eyes. Then she sat bolt upright in bed, remembering the events of the previous night.

"Paula, whatever's going on? What on earth are those dreadful smelly creatures doing in my kitchen? Get up this minute, for heaven's sake!"

Mrs Brown felt certain Paula must be at the bottom of this. What other explanation could there possibly be for the three scrawny, evil-smelling *things* so cosily installed in front of the range?

"Oh Mum," began Paula. "I had to get them. They were going to be killed. And I'd promised Minny…"

"Minny? Whoever is Minny? Paula, what *have* you been up to?"

"They're from next door, Mum. Mr Dredge keeps absolutely thousands, all locked up in cages. Oh Mum…" Paula was close to tears.

"Nonsense!" snapped Mrs Brown. "Next door's a farm, not a prison." But then she paused, frowning. "I have to say, though, they do look peculiar. Not really like hens at all."

Then Mrs Brown remembered the shock she'd just had, and that awful smell in the kitchen, and what Des would have to say any minute now… She took a deep breath: this was no moment for weakening.

"And I don't know *what* your father's going to say…" she began, but at

77

that precise moment a furious shout came from downstairs, followed by the alarming sound of Mr Brown stomping angrily up the staircase. When he appeared round Paula's bedroom door his face was a purplish-red, quite unlike its usual colour.

"What the devil's going on? What are those awful creatures doing in our kitchen? Paula, is this your idea of a joke?"

"Dad, I was trying to explain to Mum... They're from the farm. I *had* to take them. All the rest, well all the rest from sheds nine and ten, went off on these great big wagons... in the middle of the night..." Paula was crying now. Somehow she *had* to make her parents understand.

"Are you telling me you *stole* them? Good God!" Mr Brown broke off, too utterly appalled at the thought of his daughter doing something illegal to continue.

"No, I didn't steal anything. I left the money in their cage, in an envelope addressed to Mr Dredge, lots more than they were worth," sobbed Paula. "He called them rubbish."

"So, you *did* take them without permission!" roared Mr Brown.

"Yes I did," replied Paula, beginning to feel more angry than upset. "How could I let Minny down?"

"She keeps talking about someone called Minny," Mrs Brown whispered in her husband's ear. "Perhaps she's ill. You know, hallucinating or something."

"Hallucinating my foot!" snorted Mr Brown. "And those hens, if that's what those disgusting-looking creatures are, are certainly no figment of the imagination, worse luck."

"I suppose not," agreed his wife weakly.

"Get up this instant, Paula, and put your clothes on." Mr Brown glared at his daughter. "I want you downstairs in five minutes flat. You and I are taking those things back to where they belong!"

And he stormed out of the room to get dressed himself. In his fury he'd almost forgotten he was still wearing pyjamas.

"Oh Paula, what have you done?"

Mrs Brown knew she mustn't side with her daughter. Des was quite right! Of course he was! Paula couldn't possibly go around just taking things, on a whim. But she had left money, in payment; that *had* to be in

"Are you telling me you *stole* them? Good God!"

her favour. Still, the very idea! And what about Paula creeping out of the cottage while she and Des lay sound asleep? Mrs Brown turned quite pale, as she realized the implications of that. Why, *anything* could have happened to her daughter, in the dead of night. Her face softened, but she still made sure she sounded very cross indeed.

"You get dressed as quickly as you know how, and brush your hair, too. You've got to own up to all this, you know, *and* return those hens," Mrs Brown said, heading towards the door.

"Mum, there's no way I'm taking them back. Their shed's empty now. He'll only kill them," said Paula desperately.

Mrs Brown sighed. At the back of her mind she was hearing again the gentle sleepy clucking sounds that had come from those smelly, strange little creatures, when she'd first gone down to the kitchen to put the kettle on, ten long minutes ago. Peaceful, happy little sounds they'd been, quite at odds with the birds' appearance.

"Well, go round with Dad without them, first," she conceded. "The main thing is to say you're sorry, *very* sorry to Mr Dredge. Good heavens,

Paula…" Mrs Brown left the room and made her way downstairs, shaking her head. How ever had she and Des managed to produce a child who behaved in this extraordinary way?

Back in the kitchen, Mrs Brown hesitated. Instead of straightaway filling the kettle, she knelt down beside the box and the basket, and, to her own surprise, she realized she was smiling.

Minny fixed her with a beady, golden eye and clucked softly. Mrs Brown couldn't quite think how to describe the low, contented sounds made by the birds: something between a long-drawn-out cluck and a croak. And very pleasant and soothing it was, she decided.

"Well, girls," she whispered. "I simply don't know what's to become of you. I really don't."

Chapter 18

A bargain is struck

"Right, my girl!" Mr Brown wasn't looking his best, in the ill-assorted, creased clothes he'd grabbed at random from a heap on the bedroom chair; and he hadn't thought to comb his hair. Catching hold of his daughter's hand none too gently he marched her out of the cottage. Paula was pale, with eyes red from crying.

"To think a daughter of mine could steal," he raged, pulling her along at a fast pace. "Steal from next door neighbours, *and* deceive your mother and me. Creeping out in the middle of the night! As if you haven't got everything a child could possibly want for, living here. How could you *do* this, Paula?" The more Mr Brown thought about what Paula had done, the more appalled and angry he felt.

Mrs Brown had been relieved that neither her husband nor Paula had suggested she should go with them, to face the Dredges. Now she stood at the side door, watching as Mr Brown propelled Paula across the lane and up to the front door of the farmhouse. Then, with a worried frown, she turned away and went back into the warm kitchen.

"Well, girls!" Once again, she found herself talking to the hens. "Goodness only knows where it will all end. We'd certainly not expected anything like this. Perhaps moving to the country wasn't such a clever idea, after all."

Mr Brown rang the Dredges' doorbell. They could hear its ding-dong sounding inside the house, but there was no response so he pressed it again, twice this time. Paula, whose heart was thudding unpleasantly, was about to suggest they tried the kitchen door, when they heard heavy bolts being drawn back. Then the door opened a few inches, and Mrs Dredge peered out.

Her hair was untidy and hanging loose around her shoulders, and she wore a bright pink satin dressing gown with bows down the front, and fluffy pink slippers. On her face, she wore an expression of extreme annoyance.

"Yes?" Judging from her husky voice, Mrs Dredge had only just woken up, but she was alert enough to sound furious.

"We're very sorry to disturb you," began Mr Brown, "but would it be possible to speak to your husband?" Paula's father was dreading the prospect of revealing his daughter's crime; he certainly didn't want to have to go over the whole sorry story twice.

"You'll find him down in the sheds. Do you know what time it is?" Mrs Dredge snapped, slamming the door in their faces.

"Come along then, you take me there," said Mr Brown. "You're Miss Clever Clogs who knows her way around, apparently." And he half-dragged Paula in the direction of the sheds, holding her hand so tightly that it hurt.

"He's just gone in there," mumbled Paula. "Into the shed marked six. But…" She'd been about to explain about disease control, and the need to dip their boots in disinfectant, when she noticed her father was still wearing his bedroom slippers. For an awful moment she had a desire to giggle, but she just bit her lip hard, and followed her father into the annexe to shed six.

"He'll be in with the hens," Paula told her father in a small voice. "You go first."

Mr Brown stepped quickly through the gap in the big sliding door, but stopped short once inside the battery unit.

"Good Lord!" he thought, horrified. "It's gloomy in here, and noisy enough to half deafen you. And what a dreadful stink! And all these hens!" Still, he'd come with his daughter so she could apologise, hadn't he? Come to set matters right!

So, squaring his shoulders, Mr Brown began to walk purposefully in the direction of the distant figure of Mr Dredge.

"Dad!" hissed Paula, as she hurried to keep up. "We're supposed to move about slowly and quietly in here." But her father couldn't hear his daughter, above the din made by the birds.

At the alarming approach of two strangers the hens began to panic, flapping their wings, hitting them against the harsh sides of the cages. Paula and her father were leaving a trail of dust and feather particles, arising from the thousands of frightened, flapping hens. Mr Brown started to cough and splutter. Snatching a handkerchief from his pocket, he clapped it over his mouth.

They were halfway down the shed before Mr Dredge noticed the unusual rise in the noise level, and turned round. Then, his face contorted with fury, he advanced towards Mr Brown and Paula.

"What the devil...? Oh it's *you*." He stopped a few feet away, glaring at the two intruders. "You both get yourselves out of here, smartish, just look what you're doing. Upsetting my birds! This'll cost me. They'll be off-lay tomorrow, you'll see."

"I've just come to explain..." began Mr Brown.

"Well, explain away *outside* my shed," snarled Mr Dredge, and he ushered his unwanted visitors through the annexe and out into the sunshine. Paula could sense her father's relief at being back in the open air.

"Now then!" said Mr Dredge, folding his arms truculently across his chest. "Let's be hearing whatever it is you've got to say, but be quick about it. Some of us have work to do."

"I've brought my daughter here to apologise," began Mr Brown, cramming his handkerchief back into his pocket, and brushing a cobweb from his sleeve. "I'm very sorry indeed to have to say this..." Here he paused a moment, then added abruptly: "Most regrettably, she has taken three live hens from these premises. Yes, taken them from your farm." Even now, Mr Brown found his daughter's actions hard to credit.

"Pinched three of my birds? Is this true, young lady?" Mr Dredge looked thunderstruck.

"In a way it's true, but I did sort of pay for them," replied Paula.

"Pay? Pay who? Nobody paid *me*. Don't tell me one of the lads has been selling birds off on the quiet." And he narrowed his eyes suspiciously in the direction of Mike, who had just arrived for work and was parking his motor bike by the side of one of the sheds.

"Oh, no," said Paula. "I put the money in an envelope. I left it in the cage, last night, when the catchers were here." She had hoped this explanation would ease the situation but it had quite the opposite effect, for at this point Mr Dredge erupted like a long-suppressed volcano.

"That's it!" he roared. "You're coming with me into the house, the two of you. My wife will be wanting to hear about this!" And he half-pushed Mr Brown and Paula ahead of him, adding: "This could be a matter for the police, this could."

Paula felt her father's hand clench hers even harder, as all three of them hurried past the row of dreary battery sheds, towards the farmhouse, with Mr Dredge now leading the way. The kitchen door was open, and he stomped in, calling to his wife to come down immediately.

Mr Brown and Paula followed him into the kitchen. Paula looked at the clock on the wall. It was not yet half-past seven! No wonder Mrs Dredge had been so annoyed. There was no sign of Jamie; Paula guessed he would still be in bed, catching up on sleep.

"Delia!" Mr Dredge yelled to his wife again, and a moment later she could be heard making her way down the stairs. Then she appeared in the room, still wearing her pink dressing gown.

"I want a witness!" spluttered Mr Dredge. "The kid's been stealing!"

"Stealing? Stealing what?" demanded his wife, straightaway remembering a gold and diamond ring she'd carelessly left by the sink the day before. She glanced anxiously round. Ah! Thank the Lord, there it was, safe and sound.

"Hens, of course. The kid's had three of 'em already. Been snooping round when the catchers were here."

"What? Last night…?" Mrs Dredge was astonished. "You mean…?"

"We've come to apologise," broke in Mr Brown, "and to ask what Paula can do to make amends." Suddenly he felt desperate to get away.

"Paula is very sorry indeed."

Then Paula spoke, in a voice that was scarcely audible.

"Actually, Dad, I'm not sorry. Those hens were living in torment. I happen to know. You see..." she'd been about to mention the book in the library and ancestral memory, but at that moment the full force of Mr Dredge's fury broke.

"That does it! Phone the police, Delia! The kid might be young, but it's plain criminal, what she's been up to. She's just a nasty, wicked little thief!"

"I paid for them. I told you, I left all the money I've got, in an envelope, with 'Mr Dredge' written clearly on it, just where you'd be sure to find it." Now Paula was raising her voice.

"Don't be ridiculous." Mrs Dredge was reaching for her mobile. "I'm calling the police, *now*."

"Please do think again," began Mr Brown, "do let's just *all* sit down and quietly talk this thing..." but Paula cut across him.

"Go ahead," she shouted, "call the police! Ask them to come round. Then I can tell them all about the water supply! How nothing was getting through in shed 10 for a day and a half. How twenty-five thousand hens must have been half-crazy with thirst! The police just might be interested in that, and so might Save the Animals." Here Paula paused, adding quietly, "Mightn't they?" And she looked calmly at Mr Dredge, and then at his wife.

"Kid's talking rot," muttered Mr Dredge. "Absolute flaming codswallop."

There was a pause, during which all that could be heard was the ticking of the clock, and Mr Dredge's heavy breathing. Then Mrs Dredge spoke.

"Just three?" she said, trying to sound pleasant. "We'll not be missing three little hens out of that lot, surely?" She put her mobile back on the kitchen table. "Let's say we forget all about it, shall we? Just this once?" And she shot her husband a warning look.

"Well, perhaps just this time, then." Agreed Mr Dredge, attempting to re-arrange his scowl into something approaching a friendly smile. "Seeing as we're neighbours. Perhaps the little girl didn't quite understand how we go on, in the country."

"That's really very good of you," said Mr Brown, turning quickly towards the door, before the Dredges had time to change their minds. He couldn't imagine anything much worse than Paula being taken down to the police station for questioning!

"I'll send our Jamie over with a bag of layers' rations," Mr Dredge called after them. "Those birds'll be wanting what they're used to."

"Thanks," Paula called back, adding under her breath: "Pure garbage, actually, from a hen's point of view."

Mr Brown gave his daughter an odd look, but decided to say nothing. Right now, he was feeling an urgent need for a large, hot, strong cup of coffee, with at least three lumps of sugar in it. Seeing inside that battery place, he was thinking, it's quite shaken me up. Knocked the stuffing clean out of me. Why, you could have cut the atmosphere in there with a knife, that awful feeling of stress coming from those birds… Well, it just couldn't be right, could it?

Paula and her father retraced their steps to Orchard Cottage in silence. Mr Brown was still holding his daughter's hand, but now it was in a soft, warm way. Rather to his surprise, he found himself thinking about those little scraps by the kitchen range; he was wondering roughly how big an enclosure would have to be, to keep them happy? And what kind of hut would they need, for roosting in at night?

Still, he reflected, they'll obviously have to stay in the garage for quite a while, a few weeks, most likely, with some kind of heater on night and day; at least one of them was missing too many feathers to survive without extra warmth, certainly at this time of year.

"Well, a spot of breakfast wouldn't be such a bad idea," he said, letting go of Paula's hand. "Why don't you go on ahead and tell your mum we're on our way?"

And Paula ran up the garden path, her heart singing.

Chapter 19
Minny has her doubts

After his big cup of strong, sweet coffee and a couple of slices of toast, Mr Brown phoned Uncle Ian to say he'd be an hour or two late in for work. Then he sorted out some planks of wood he found stacked away behind the garden shed, and with these fenced off a corner in the garage.

"Good thing there's a power point handy," he called over his shoulder, as he hurried out to the car. "They'll need a heat lamp. Be back as soon as I can. I'm just off to buy one, and a bale of straw and what-not."

"Thank heavens your dad's not still angry," said Mrs Brown as soon as she heard the door close behind him. "He's being really good about all this."

"It's because he saw inside that place," said Paula, adding: "That's so, isn't it Minny?"

Minny gave Paula a conspiratorial look, but merely clucked. She hadn't spoken a word since last night.

"If only she could talk!" laughed Mrs Brown. "She'd have some tales to tell. Not that we'd have time to listen to them, just at the moment. It looks like we've a busy day ahead of us, sorting these girls out. Just clear the table, will you love, while I go and get dressed. I'm the only one in this family still in my dressing gown."

"OK, Mum."

Once her mother was out of the room Paula went and knelt beside Minny's basket. "Not long now, Minny, I promise," she said, adding: "Hen's honour."

"One can only hope not," replied Minny. She was clearly trying to sound cheerful, but she had a tense look about her.

"Is something wrong?" Paula felt a sudden stab of fear. What if Minny were ill? What if she should die, before her first-ever chance of freedom?

"I'm just worried. Worried sick, in fact," replied Minny. "You see…"

The little hen paused, then she went on: "You see, I may well prove to be institutionalised. Seriously, indeed permanently, institutionalised."

"Whatever do you mean?" asked Paula, not at all sure of the meaning of the last, long word.

"Well," explained Minny, "I've spent all my life in an institution of sorts, have I not? Lights on for hours on end to pretend it's summer, eggs rolling away the moment they're laid, no chance even to walk about, let alone make meaningful decisions about preening, dust bathing, scratching around in a sensible place… The list of deprivations is endless." Minny's voice trailed off miserably.

"But Minny! Remember your dreams."

"Ah, my dreams. That's precisely why I'm so frightened. Suppose I can't act out my dreams? Not tomorrow, perhaps not ever," Minny finished sadly.

"Of course you'll be able to!" said Paula, sounding more confident than she felt. "My dad will be back soon, with a big bale of straw, and a lamp to hang over your new home so you won't feel the cold. Any minute now your dreams will really start to come true!"

"Well, I only hope you're right," replied Minny, still sounding upset. "I'm not at all sure I could survive a major disappointment. Not now. Life's been so very hard."

"Ancestral memory," Paula whispered in a comforting voice. "That will *never* let you down."

"Paula!" Mrs Brown was calling from upstairs. "It's time you were dressed. Properly, I mean. And what about a quick bath?" Mrs Brown had detected that certain musty smell again, and noticed it on Des, too.

Smiling, Paula stacked the breakfast things onto the draining board, whispered "See you, Minny", then, calling: "Coming, Mum", she bounded upstairs, two at a time.

Chapter 20
New beginnings

"Wasn't that good of your dad?" Mrs Brown was standing at the kitchen window, watching her husband back the car out into the lane. He was leaving, exactly three hours late, for Uncle Ian's garage. "He's sorted out a really cosy corner for those hens. A heat lamp and everything. A proper little five star hotel!"

"Dad's been great," agreed Paula.

Paula and her mother had been having elevenses. Installing the hens in their new home had been hard work, and breakfast had, by Mrs Brown's standards, been a rather snatched affair. And now Paula was desperate to go out to the garage, to see how Minny and the others were settling into their new home.

She took a gulp of tea and pushed her chair back from the table. "I've had enough, Mum, I'm going to see how they're getting on."

"All right, love, you go along," smiled Mrs Brown. She was remembering her first kitten, when she was a child, the way that fluffy black and white scrap had seemed the most important thing in the world. "I can see Jamie coming our way, carrying a big bag."

"It'll be the hens' food." Paula grabbed her coat and headed for the door. "See you, Mum. Jamie'll help me sort the hens out. He should know what to do!"

"Hi, Jamie!"

"Hi!" Jamie was pale from lack of sleep. "Dad says the hens ought to have this for a few days, 'cause they've never known anything else."

"Thanks for bringing it round," said Paula. "Do you want to see the girls?"

"'Course," said Jamie, "I *was* rather involved in their rescue, remember? Where have you put them? I bet they're not still in your kitchen!"

"Dad's made them a sort of temporary home, in the garage. Actually, it's wicked." Paula was feeling proud of her father.

"He's stopped being furious, then? My dad said your dad was mega-mad with you. You know, for taking the hens." Jamie paused a moment, then added, with a puzzled look, "Then for some odd reason, *my* dad seemed to decide to forget all about it."

"Well, I did just happen to mention the water supply. Or rather the lack of it." Paula tried hard not to look smug. "Don't worry, though, you've not been involved. And you never will be, not ever."

"Phew!" said Jamie. "Thanks for that!"

"Come and see, then."

Quietly, Paula opened the door into the garage, and the two crept inside.

A lamp, suspended a few feet above the hens, cast a warm glow over the scene, and Mr Brown, with Paula's help, had covered the floor in the fenced off area with a layer of fresh straw. In one corner stood a water container specially designed for poultry (Mr Brown had bought it that morning at the Farm Supplies shop) and Mrs Brown had broken the end of a loaf into little pieces and scattered the crumbs into the straw.

Nearby in the garage was a fat roll of carpet, intended for Paula's bedroom once it had been re-decorated, and this made a comfortable seat. Intrigued, Paula and Jamie sat down on it to watch.

The three hens looked so very strange! Only Crosspatch had a proper covering of feathers, and those were raggedy and dull. Goldie had a few strong wing feathers, just enough to prove that she'd once been beautiful. But Minny! Well, Minny verged on the absolutely naked!

Her skin was pink and pimply, where feathers should have been, and her tail end was an angry red. Paula was shocked to see a large lump at the base of Minny's long neck.

"Whatever's that?" she whispered, pointing fearfully.

"That's just her crop. It's where their food gets ground up," explained Jamie.

"It looks awful, with no feathers to cover it up. I hope they'll all grow again."

"I don't know. Most prob'ly they will." Jamie was frowning. He couldn't imagine Minny ever looking like a proper hen.

Just now, Minny was tentatively exploring the enclosure, picking her feet up cautiously, holding each one poised high in the air for a second or two before placing it down again, a little further forward.

"Minny's teaching herself to walk," Paula breathed. "She's finding out she can actually *get* somewhere if she puts one foot in front of the other."

"And look at old Crosspatch," said Jamie, "She's having fun all right!"

Crosspatch was using her legs and feet properly for the first time. Head down, she was vigorously kicking straw out behind her, in an exciting quest for Mrs Brown's breadcrumbs.

Suddenly, Goldie crouched down in a corner and started to contort her body, twisting this way and that. Paula stared at her in horror.

"Whatever's the matter with Goldie? She looks like she's gone mad, or something!"

Jamie laughed. "Oh, she's OK. She's just having a dust bath. She's been waiting a whole year for this."

"How do you know what she's doing?"

"'Cause I've seen my friend Andrew's hens doing it, lots of times. It cleans their feathers. Hardly worth it with Goldie, though, the amount she's got."

"It must be ancestral memory. Minny told me..." Paula stopped abruptly, blushing scarlet. For an instant she caught Minny's bright eye, but the little hen just started busying herself in the straw. To cover her embarrassment, Paula hurried on, "I expect she wants to smarten herself up a bit. But it does look *gross*, all that writhing about, with half her feathers missing. Well, more than half, actually," she rattled on.

"Poor thing," said Jamie. Then he turned to Paula, his eyes shining.

"Hey! I haven't told you the good news!"

"Go on, then," said Paula, hugely relieved that her reference to Minny as a source of information seemed to have passed unnoticed.

"Dad's giving up the hens. For good. He says they're losing him money."

"Cool! Oh, *totally* cool, Jamie." Paula felt herself turning red again, but with delight this time. "When? You mean now? *Right* now?"

"Well, not exactly straight away. You know, he'll have to go on for a few months. Till they're all old, I suppose. You know, till..." Jamie didn't want to spell it out.

"I know," said Paula quietly, thinking sadly of the long weeks ahead for the thousands of hens still imprisoned in Mr Dredge's cages, imagining them waking up every morning to face another day of misery. Then an alarming thought came to her. "But you don't mean you're moving? Not leaving the farm?"

"No way," said Jamie firmly. "Mum and Dad have got great plans, apparently. All hatched behind my back, of course."

"Of course," said Paula sympathetically. "They do that."

"Mushrooms," Jamie went on.

"*Mushrooms?*" Paula was puzzled.

"In the sheds!" replied Jamie, triumphantly. "Mushrooms grow in the dark, apparently. Dad's got all this information. You should see our kitchen. There are leaflets about how to grow mushrooms all over the place."

"Well, at least mushrooms can't feel." Paula stopped herself from saying more. After all, Mr and Mrs Dredge *were* Jamie's parents.

"Now the two end sheds are empty," Jamie went on, "they can make a start. Mum's planning a farm shop. You know, selling things they've grown themselves. Well, Dad'll do the growing. Mum's fingernails would break off if *she* tried. She's just going to organise everything."

"Wow! That'll be convenient for my mum. A shop right next door!"

"The one problem is, poor old Prince will have to go," said Jamie frowning. "Dad says having a chained up Alsatian barking blue murder wouldn't exactly encourage the punters. And Mum won't allow a dog inside the house."

Paula felt a stab of anxiety. Surely the Dredges wouldn't have Prince put to sleep, just because he didn't fit in with their new plans? She was remembering his golden eyes, and his poor matted-up tail thumping when he'd realized she wanted to be friends.

Just then Jamie's excited voice broke into her thoughts.

"Look, Paula! Minny's making herself a nest!"

They watched, spellbound. Minny was picking up strands of straw in her beak, and confidently forming them into a definite shape. First she turned to one side, then the other, skilfully building her nest. Higher and higher it went, until Minny herself was almost hidden from sight.

"She's making up for lost time," said Jamie, amused.

"She'll be wanting to lay an egg soon," said Paula. "Perhaps we'd better leave her in peace. They like somewhere a bit secret for their eggs. Dad's going to make them a proper nesting box at the weekend."

Jamie shot Paula a strange look. Once more, he was thinking his new friend seemed to know an awful lot about hens, especially for a complete townie.

"OK," he agreed. "I'll just put some of the food in with them. Then they'll have everything they need."

"Mum's donated a dish," said Paula. "It's nice and heavy, so they won't tip it up." She got up from the carpet roll and fetched an old earthenware crock, and Jamie filled it with the mealy mixture the hens were used to. The word 'garbage' crossed Paula's mind, but she said not a word.

Then Paula and Jamie paused for a moment, for one last look at the contented hens.

The main part of the garage was in near-darkness; just the fenced-off corner glowed warmly in the golden light that shone down on the yellow straw, and onto the three lucky hens. The only sounds to disturb the peaceful silence were occasional low clucks, and the rustle of straw.

Once outside, the two friends blinked in the bright sunshine. The weather had turned warmer, and fleecy clouds flecked a sky of speedwell blue. In a few days, a mass of wild daffodils would be gleaming under the old fruit trees in the orchard.

"Come on, Jamie," said Paula, closing the garage door quietly. "Let's go and tell my mum about Minny's nest."

"And about Goldie's first dust bath," laughed Jamie.

"And about Crosspatch kicking the straw about with her great big feet!" added Paula.

And they went running into the cottage, to look for Mrs Brown.

Chapter 21
Dreams come true

It was high summer in the garden of Orchard Cottage. Back in May and June, in long-forgotten flowerbeds, masses of Granny's Bonnets had appeared as if from nowhere, nodding their many-coloured heads amidst clumps of forget-me-nots, to be followed by poppies, lavenders and delphiniums. And now old roses and honeysuckles, still dormant when the Browns had arrived in early spring, clambered over walls and peeped in at upstairs windows.

Fortunately, Mr Brown had been far too busy decorating the cottage to even think about digging, and he'd mostly left the garden well alone. But Mrs Brown had done wonders, weeding and pruning, and staking up newly discovered plants with loving care. Now they were outside the cottage as dusk was falling and bats flitted about in the summery air, sitting on their newly-acquired garden seat and drinking in the peaceful scene.

"Well, Des, I didn't have to wait for my little bit of heaven after all," Mrs Brown commented. "It seems it was right here, all along."

"Absolutely," agreed Mr Brown, sniffing the night-scented stock appreciatively. "Still plenty to do, of course, but you couldn't want for more. Not this evening."

The following morning, hot sunshine streamed into the kitchen, highlighting the scarlet and pink of the geraniums that crowded every windowsill. Mrs Brown was sorting out some scraps for the hens, thinking how nothing much was wasted these days, in the Brown household.

And now Paula came clattering down the stairs into the kitchen; today was the first day of the summer holidays.

From the kitchen window, she could see Minny,
Goldie and Crosspatch, all fully feathered now,
pecking around in the grassy orchard.

"Jamie'll be coming round in a bit," she said. "We're going to make a camp, at the top of the orchard."

"Good idea," said Mrs Brown. "Take this up to the hens when you go, will you? I've saved some of their favourites."

Paula peered into the old enamel dish her mother was holding. "Rice and melon seeds. Yummy! Well, yummy if you happen to be a hen. Thanks, Mum."

"Here comes Jamie now," said Mrs Brown.

"I'll go out and meet him," said Paula, taking the dish. "See you later."

"Yes, love, see you later."

Mrs Brown stood watching as Paula and Jamie greeted each other, then strolled off across the lawn.

They're certainly very good friends, she thought happily. And thank goodness we're all making the best of the Dredges, after that terrible start.

From the kitchen window she could just make out Minny, Goldie and Crosspatch, all fully feathered now, pecking around in the grassy orchard. When Paula and Jamie were only halfway up the garden, the hens spotted them and, with wings outspread, all three half ran, half flew towards them, eager for their treat.

Mrs Brown smiled, and turned away from the window. Her kitchen was just as she wanted it now, especially on such a bright sunny morning.

"Well," she said aloud, "I think we can say the Browns' move to the country turned out to be a thoroughly good thing, all round."

And from his favourite place beside the kitchen range Prince thumped his tail lazily, in complete agreement.

Printed in Great Britain
by Amazon.co.uk, Ltd.,
Marston Gate.